WHITE BEFORE CHRISTMAS

Sunflower ROSE
PUBLISHING

Cover Design by Jared Roach at DRMR Creative

Editing by: Bianca Shakur at B.Edits

Cover Art by freepik

ISBN: 979-8-9894618-2-0

To everyone that needs a little extra magic this Christmas.

Prologue
Fifty-Three Years Ago

"Come sit by this tree, Amada. I have a gift for you." Twenty-two-year-old Amada Wright glanced up from the book she was reading and smiled at her grandmother, Ella. Even as a young adult, when most of her peers were off spending time with friends and significant others, Amada preferred to spend her Christmases with her grandmother. The woman who raised her after her parents tragically died in a car accident.

Amada stood up and sat by the Christmas tree, as Ella had requested. She watched as her grandmother, weathered and worn with age, stooped under the tree and grabbed a box. It was rectangular and covered in sparkly gold ribbon.

"Thank you, Grammy. You didn't have to do this I-" Amada began.

"Hush and open it, child." Ella interrupted with a wide smile. Amada chuckled and tugged on the ribbon. It unraveled to show a hasty tape job. Ella was never skilled at wrapping gifts. She covered the box in tape and ill-shapen paper, hoping that would suffice. Amada ran her finger under one of the looser ends and popped the box open. Inside lay a leather-bound journal with a feathered quill pen resting against it. Amada's eyes lit. Her grandmother knew how much she loved to write.

"Oh," she gushed, "Grammy, this journal is lovely."

"This isn't just a regular journal, my sweet granddaughter." Her grandmother said, sinking back onto the couch. She patted the spot next to her, motioning for Amada to join her. "This journal is special."

"How?" Amada asked, turning it over in her hands. To her, as gorgeous as it was, it still resembled a regular journal. There were no special markings on the outer cover. Just plain black leather. She opened it to look at the pages.

"This journal is what brought your grandfather to me."

Amada remained quiet, waiting for Ella to explain, but she stayed silent for a moment, tears welling in her eyes. Only two years had passed since his untimely death, but it still felt as recent as today. Ella had been inconsolable when the love of her life breathed his last breath.

Ella sighed heavily and blinked away the tears. Amada watched as her grandmother turned towards her and grabbed her hands. "This journal is magic."

"Magic?"

"Yes. It's magic. My grandmother gave it to me long ago and when she did, I met your grandfather a month later. That man loved me harder than anyone has ever loved me. I want the same for you." Ella said, squeezing Amada's hands gently.

"I'm sure it's just a coincidence that- "

"No, Amada, it's not a coincidence." Ella picked up the book. "You will see. This pen and this journal work together to write a love story for whomever it chooses. It has chosen you."

"How?" Amada asked.

"You ask too many questions, child. Listen to your Grammy. My grandmother gave me this book, saying it would hold my love story. And it did."

"Then why is it still blank?"

"When it's the next person's turn, the previous story in it erases." Ella seemed so sure of what she was saying, even though none of it made any sense. A magical pen and journal that writes your own love story? It seemed far-fetched at best, and completely unheard of at worst, but she didn't want to make her grandmother feel badly.

"Okay, Grammy. Whatever you say." Amada smiled. "Can you please open the present I brought for you now? She wasn't certain what else to say, so she settled on changing the subject completely. Ella studied Amada for a moment, searching her eyes for something. Finally, she agreed and forced a smile of her own.

"Sure, baby," she said.

Amada disregarded the defeat in her grandmother's tone and grabbed the hidden box from under the tree. Inside was a delicate cross pendant with a round sapphire in the middle. "It's breathtaking!"

Pride coursed through Amada at her grandmother's reaction to the jewelry. She had been hunting for a perfect gift for months. It had been hard to top the gifts her grandfather had given Ella. Amada lovingly remembered the Christmas when her grandfather had decorated the entire house while Ella had been sleeping. When she woke up, her favorite dinner was being prepared.

Despite their limited finances, Amada's grandfather always made sure his two cherished women felt loved. Just behind Ella's joyful facade, Amada sensed her lingering pain over her husband's loss.

Amada had grown up watching the two of them behave like newlyweds. She had always wanted a relationship similar to the one her grandparents had. The few she tried lacked the spark she saw within her grandparents.

Her eyes wandered to the journal and the pen resting on the couch next to Ella. The idea that these two mundane, everyday items could direct her toward her own great love was a fun thought. Even if it was impossible. Ella followed Amada's focused gaze and smiled at the journal.

"I know what I'm saying doesn't make a lick of sense, child. I didn't believe my grandma when she told me, either. I believed she was crazy. I'm sure you're thinking the same thing."

Amada shook her head. "I could never think such thoughts about you, Grammy."

"Listen to what I'm telling you. This will give you your own love story. A mighty one. And when it's done, when you have found your love, it will tell you who to give it to next. Don't ask questions. Just follow instructions. Do you hear me, child?" Ella demanded. Amada nodded, still skeptical, but not wanting to disappoint her grandmother. Ella picked up the book and pressed it against Amada's chest.

"Your own great love story, just you wait and see."

1

Elodie

"Ms. Banks! Are you going to give us homework over Thanksgiving break?" I looked up from my desk and made a face at Kellan, one of my most rambunctious students. He constantly yelled across the classroom instead of speaking in a regular tone, as if the room wasn't small enough for me to hear him normally.

"If you don't stop yelling in my classroom, then yes, I will," I said, crossing my arms over my chest.

Kellan flushed red and shrugged. "Sorry, Ms. B," he said with his famous crooked grin.

I raised an eyebrow at him and glanced down at my watch. Three o'clock. Just thirty more minutes until I can finally escape my students for a few days. I loved being a teacher, but it was not an undemanding job. Some of these students were skilled in finding my last nerve and stomping it into the ground daily. Audacity is always in season with this bunch but, in my five years teaching English Language Arts to seventh and eighth graders, this was my favorite group of students, even if they drove me crazy sometimes.

Even though it was strictly against the rules of my classroom, students lined up in front of the door, waiting for the bell that signals their escape to ring. Usually, I would tell them to sit back down and wait until I dismissed them, but I understood the excitement this time. It was Tuesday, two days before Thanksgiving, and they were out until the following Monday. I eagerly anticipated the few days of sleeping in. My favorite part of the holidays. I had promised my grandmother that I would come over and help her cook this Thanksgiving, so I knew my Wednesday and Thursday mornings would be full of cooking and prepping with the family's matriarch, but that still left Friday and the weekend for me to catch up on some sleep.

The loud chime of the bell brought me out of my thoughts just in time to see all of my kids trying to shove their way out of the classroom door at one time. I shook my head at the pile-up. This is why I tell them to wait until I dismiss them, so they don't all get stuck in the door trying to be the first one out.

"Relax! One at a time!" I called over the noise.

Classrooms across the hall opened and students from other grades and subjects spilled out into the hallway, chattering excitedly. It was one of my favorite parts of the day if no students were fighting; watching them connect with their friends always put a smile on my face.

As the final student left, I sighed and returned to my desk. My manuscript was on my laptop in front of me. The same manuscript I had been working on for months. I tried countless times to rework the scenes, but the plot still didn't flow as I wished.

"Hey, El. You got car duty today?" The fifth-grade math teacher, Alex Watkins, poked his head in my classroom. His shaggy blonde hair fell over his eyes, making him look more like a student than a math teacher. We went on a few dates, but we were better as friends. If he had his way, we would already be married and expecting our first child together. Or at least engaged. I would often catch him staring at me when he didn't think I was looking. It had started as endearing, but now it's bordering on creepy. I deeply regretted letting our relationship move past the friends' stage, even briefly.

"Hey, Alex. No, not today. I was just looking at my manuscript before I wrap things up and go home." Teachers with car duty had to stick around to make sure all the students got in the correct vehicles. The teachers alternated weeks, so no one was stuck doing it more than the others. It was not a fun task, especially during the hotter months. Thankfully, today was not my turn. The heavy winds outside made the frigid air even more intense.

Alex stepped further into the classroom and looked at the book peeking out of my purse.

"The Souls of Black Folk." He murmured, reading the title scrawled across the spine of the book. He nodded like he was familiar with the book. It was the collection of essays by W.E. B Dubois that I had been studying. I'm sure administration would be upset with me for having this book with me, but black literature deserves a space in the classroom. I hadn't yet figured out how to incorporate something so specific into my curriculum, but I was working on it. These kids had to learn about these books somehow.

"What are your Thanksgiving plans?" he asked as I slipped my purse over my shoulder. He quickly fell into step beside me as we both made our way to the parking lot. He'd made a habit of walking me out to my car every day and even though it was sweet, I didn't need it.

"The family is going over to my grandma's house for Thanksgiving. Usual routine. I offered to help with the cooking this year, which will be something different. What are you guys doing?"

Alex shrugged. "My family doesn't really cook. So, I'll probably just watch movies."

I felt bad listening to Alex talk about how his family didn't do much to celebrate the holidays. Thanksgiving and Christmas were always huge deals in my family. The planning would start months in advance. The menu for Christmas had already been circulated through our emails and family group chats before the end of October.

I considered inviting him, but that would send an undesired message to both Alex and my family. I already knew my family would give me a mean side-eye if I brought a man over for the holidays. No amount of denying would convince them he and I weren't together. He and I were just friends, nothing more. That was a can of worms I really didn't want to open until I was ready to introduce them to someone truly special.

"Maybe you guys should start some new traditions?" I offered. "That's half the fun."

Alex glanced around the parking lot, waving at the last few lingering students and teachers. I waved at a few myself. This school was the first where I truly felt like part of a family. What this school system lacked in salary; it made up for in the community.

"Ms. Banks! Can I have a quick word with you before you go?!" I glanced behind Alex to see Principal Ardell walking briskly towards us, clutching a slip of paper. Her pencil heels clicked on the concrete with each step.

"Sure. Is everything okay?" I asked warily. It wasn't every day that Principal Ardell wanted to speak with me. She usually kept to herself in her office with the door closed, only coming out occasionally to discipline an unruly student or check in with the classrooms closest to her. It gave her an air of intimidation. Most of us were terrified of getting on her bad side. Our jobs depended on whether she was satisfied with our performance. She nodded a quick greeting at Alex and focused her attention back on me.

"Yes, it's nothing pressing. I just wanted to catch you before you left so you'd have enough time to begin. Walk with me?" Her request left little room for protest. Alex touched my arm as a goodbye and headed towards his vehicle. He'd probably try to text me later to see what the conversation was about. I followed Principal Ardell, taking in her entire outfit. She amazed everyone by effortlessly walking on stiletto heels all day. My feet would be screaming for release after three hours.

She wore black palazzo pants with a white pinstriped blouse tucked in at the waist. Her auburn locs were twisted into an intricate updo that allowed her sharp cheekbones to show. Her russet skin was smooth and glistened even in the setting sun. She had the nerve to look freshly moisturized in this freezing cold air. Male teachers openly gawked at Principal Ardell while a few women did the same. I suspected she was aware of being the subject of their fantasies, but professionalism prevented her from acknowledging it. As long as everyone remained respectful it wouldn't be an issue.

I admired Principal Ardell. Her beauty played second fiddle to her brains. She was incredibly smart and earned her PhD in education much faster than was considered normal. It made me, someone still awkwardly flailing through life, feel inadequate in my pursuit of a solid career. I aspired to match her composure, but my wild curls and tendency to stumble over nothing made it nearly impossible.

"So, as you know," she began, "We are due to begin practicing for our Christmas musical as soon as the kids come back from Thanksgiving break." Every year, Astoria Middle puts on a Christmas production. It's a huge deal in the community because all the proceeds go towards a charity or program that we sponsor. More attendees mean more funds to donate after the event. Last year, our production helped the local homeless shelter provide meals for the holiday season.

"Right. It's usually the talk of the town. Mrs. Blumenthal is supposed to be handling the music this year, correct?" The last bus of kids pulled away, leaving Principal Ardell and me in the parking lot by ourselves. She paused briefly, shifting her stance from one foot to the other.

"That's what I wanted to talk to you about, actually..."

"Oh?" My eyebrows shot up.

"Yes. Mrs. Blumenthal had a death in the family and won't be back for some time. I was wondering if you would mind working with the new music teacher for the play this year, Mr. Davis. He has had some experience being the background musician for a Tustin Jimberlake? Maybe you've heard of him. I think his talent could really bring in a lot of donations this year."

"First, why is he teaching here if he's so famous?" I asked, tilting my head to one side. "And second, this is incredibly short notice."

She gave a curt nod. "Apologies, but I'm confident the change will be good. Please! I am slightly desperate. No one else is willing to step in if you decide not to."

"Wow, what a way to make me feel special, but luckily for you, I love Christmas," I replied with a smile. Principal Ardell's facial expression softened with relief.

"Oh, thank God! This has been extremely stressful for me. Have you met Mr. Davis yet?"

Mekhi Davis joined the school a short time ago, after the previous music teacher left for another school. I had only seen him briefly, and we hadn't talked yet. But, according to the teachers, he was attractive and reserved.

"No, I haven't met him yet, but Alyssa and Moriah talk about him constantly. Said he's rather fun to look at." I replied with a shrug. Principal Ardell rolled her eyes.

"How is it possible to be that boy crazy as an adult?" she muttered.

I smiled. Those two spent every waking moment they weren't teaching, giggling and obsessing about men. Alyssa, with her thin brown hair and pale freckled skin, had a different boyfriend every month.

Principal Ardell handed me the slip of paper she was holding. "Here is how you can reach Mr. Davis. I figured you two would need to get started as soon as possible. He's aware of your participation."

"But you weren't even aware of my participation until a few minutes ago." I narrowed my eyes. "Did you just play me?"

A mischievous grin brightened her regal features. "I would never. Thank you so much for helping, Elodie. I owe you one." She turned on her heel and headed back towards the school. I started toward my parking space, wondering if I would end up regretting agreeing to help with the program this year. In the past, I assisted, but never led. Despite her genius for teaching songs quickly, Mrs. Blumenthal would always be extra stressed during Christmas.

I slipped inside my car, relishing the brief moment of silence. My mind drifted back to my manuscript, trying fruitlessly to sort out the kinks while I drove out of the parking lot and towards home. I knew I needed to try to work on it tonight after my shift at the homeless shelter if I wanted to have something to give to my editor by the deadline, but my brain felt mushy and useless. Maybe working on the Christmas musical would give me something to take my mind off the story. My best ideas always popped up when I wasn't thinking about it.

The sound of my phone ringing echoed through my Toyota. I glanced at the screen. It was Deja. One of my best friends from college. A group of us had met during freshman year and remained tight knit, even as we branched off into other degrees and then career fields. Deja was in marketing and was the first person on my list to call whenever I got this book together.

I picked up on the second ring. "Hey Deja."

"Hey girl. Are we still on for the Novel-Tea meeting tomorrow night?" she asked. Novel-Tea, the book club we started in college, was one of my brightest spots during the week. It forces us to break away from our personal lives at least once a week to catch up and talk about books. Being the most bookish, I eagerly anticipated the chance to brainstorm ideas for my novel and it gave me a chance to reconnect with my four closest friends.

"Absolutely. Did you finish the book?" I pulled into my driveway, thankful to be home. Spending so much time standing and walking around always exhausted my body. My bladder was screaming at me to get to the nearest bathroom.

"No. I'm powering through it right now. We've had an intense week at the firm with the holidays coming up. Seems like all our clients want to launch campaigns at the same time." Deja sighed.

She ran her own marketing firm on the other side of town. A prominent name in the city, it served clients from massive companies and rival renowned firms in the state. It was impressive for someone who was still in their early thirties. She juggled so much, I couldn't fathom how she found time to sleep, let alone read.

"Do you think Audrey will make some of her famous Philly Cheesesteak roll-ups?" I asked, reaching to grab my stuff out of the passenger seat. "I've been craving more since she brought some to the last meeting."

"She might, but I already put in my order for her zucchini fries, so you may have to wait until the next go around."

I made a face. Zucchini fries weren't on my list of book club treats, but I would try it. More than likely, I would steal a few bites while I was helping my grandmother cook for Thanksgiving and would be too full to even eat zucchini fries.

"Fine, but if I don't like them, I'm blaming you for ruining book club snacks."

"Since when do you hate anything Audrey makes?" Deja shot back. "You end up finishing off whatever it is she brings. Don't act brand new." We both laughed. It was rare that I didn't like something Audrey had created in the kitchen. I likely would've eaten more vegetables as a child, if she was there. She had been cooking since she was young and had turned that skill into a paycheck when we graduated from college.

"Speaking of nasty food, I agreed to work at the homeless shelter tonight." I unlocked my front door and tossed my bag on the nearest chair. The pumpkin spice air freshener I had just installed before I left that morning made my house smell like a yummy bakery. I couldn't stand the taste of pumpkin spice, but the smell was enough to remind me of the fall season. "I wanted to get my day in before the holiday because I already know tomorrow is going to be crazy. You coming with me?"

"Not if you expect me to finish this book."

After getting off the phone with Deja, I glanced at the clock. I only had a few minutes to get to the homeless shelter. Even though I wanted to cancel out of pure exhaustion, it was something I promised myself I would do every year. I changed out of my work clothes and put on one of my more comfortable Christmas sweaters and headed back out to my car.

When I arrived at the shelter, they were getting ready to serve. A small group lined up, anticipating entry. I smiled at the head attendant, Victor, and made my way to the kitchen to grab an apron and a hairnet. Stuffing all of my hair into this tiny hairnet was always a task.

"These are supposed to be stretchy!" I muttered. I knew I should have attempted to tie my hair back in a more manageable pineapple or a ponytail at the nape of my neck, but I had been too preoccupied to remember.

"Elodie?" a deep voice said from behind me. I turned, expecting to see Victor, but Mekhi stood in the doorway of the kitchen, watching me with a mildly amused expression. I sucked in a breath. Alyssa and Moriah were absolutely correct. He was unfairly attractive.

"What are you doing here?" I asked, surprised.

"Volunteering." He replied, reaching around me for another hairnet. The fabric of his cream-colored sweater stretched against his arms with the movement. The color looked gorgeous against his umber skin. I stared, bewildered, as he grabbed another hairnet, placed it over his glistening beard, and looped it over his ears. The gesture was distracting for some reason. I found myself tracking each of his movements with my eyes. "You good?"

His question made me realize I was openly gawking at him. I had glimpsed him before, but this is my first opportunity to fully observe his appearance. I couldn't believe someone this gorgeous slipped past me without being noticed. For the last two weeks, I had been coming to work every day with this adonis in the same building. Shouldn't there have been an announcement or a smoke signal of some kind? I hadn't been putting my best foot forward with my outfits. Had I known there was now someone in the school worth impressing, I would have been pulling out all the stops.

"I-Yes... I'm fine. Sorry," I cleared my throat and smoothed my suddenly sweaty hands down the front of my apron. I was thankful he couldn't read minds, so he wouldn't know how dirty my thoughts had suddenly become. "Should we get started?"

Mekhi smiled at me; his eyes twinkling. "Lead the way."

2

Mekhi

I almost didn't come tonight. I had been so tired after work and looking forward to relaxing before the excitement of the Thanksgiving holiday; I had almost called Victor and told him I wouldn't be able to help tonight. Reluctantly, I made my way to the homeless shelter, with the goal of fulfilling my duties and departing. What I didn't expect, however, was to see Elodie standing in the kitchen struggling to stuff her curls into a hairnet.

"Do you volunteer here a lot?" I asked, grabbing a pan of candied yams and carrying it out to the serving station. Elodie followed behind me with a pan of turkey. Victor bustled around the room making sure everything was in order.

"Not as often as I'd like. What about you?"

"Whenever I'm not on the road, I try to make it here a few times. Especially around the holiday season."

The line in front of the plates was growing by the second. I hoped we had enough food to make sure everyone had their fill. Knowing Victor, there were extra pans of everything in the back. Soft holiday music played in the background, giving the cafeteria-style room a homier feel.

"So, any thoughts about this Christmas production we've both been roped into?" Elodie asked, the corner of her mouth tilted upwards in a small smile. Truth was, I had thought about the musical. Ever since Principal Ardell told me that Elodie would be helping me put the production together, my mind has been buzzing with the possibilities.

I'd seen her in the halls during my first few weeks of teaching at the school, and each time I laid eyes on her, my breath would catch in my throat. This woman is gorgeous. Smooth caramel skin, big brown eyes, full lips, and curves visible even through her obnoxious Christmas sweater; it was a wonder that she wasn't being hit on daily. I could write an entire album off her eyes alone. The same expressive brown eyes that were staring at me right now.

"Mekhi?" She tilted her head, a loose curl brushing the side of her face. It took everything in me not to reach up and tuck it behind her ear. I blinked, not realizing I had completely blanked out of the conversation.

"Uh, yes. I have a song list in mind. Nothing super complicated, just a few songs that the kids will hopefully enjoy." I scooped a hearty serving of yams on the plate of the man standing in front of me with a smile. "Happy Thanksgiving, sir."

He shifted to stand in front of Elodie, waiting for turkey and ignoring me completely.

"Don't be stingy with the turkey, girl," the man patted his stomach. "I need enough food to hold me over."

She made a show of looking around the room before placing another two slices on his plate with a wink. The man grinned at her. I couldn't help but watch the exchange, in awe of Elodie's ease with people. Others were gravitating towards her even after they had received their food, looking for conversation or just wanting to be near her. She had a light that drew people in. That was rare in an environment like this, with people who were so used to darkness. A few more people passed through the line before she turned back to me.

"Is the piano the only instrument you can play?" She asked, diverting her gaze from me to the table. She absentmindedly scooped a serving of green beans onto someone's plate and smiled warmly at them. I watched her, taking a moment to memorize everything I could about her. When she turned her gaze back to me, I shook my head.

"No. I can play a few others."

"Which ones are your favorite?"

"The piano and the saxophone have the best sound, in my opinion. Makes them the most fun." I served the man standing in front of me, carefully scooping the mashed potatoes onto his overflowing plate. He nodded gratefully and moved further down the line.

"I look forward to hearing what you have." It was a simple statement, but it sent a jolt of electricity through my spine. I nodded and swallowed the lump forming in my throat. I didn't want to admit how excited I was to spend some extra time with her, but I was. Just like the others in this room, I wanted more of her light. I wanted to experience her in a different, more intimate way. Just standing next to her now, wordlessly scooping yams onto plates, made my knees wobble a little.

After everyone had eaten their fill, we cleaned up what was left. Some servers packed up the food that was left and handed it out to anyone who wanted an extra plate. I glanced at my watch. It was a little after ten o'clock and normally I would be ready to call it a night after teaching and volunteering, but I felt unusually energized.

"What are your plans for the rest of the night?" I asked Elodie as I walked her to her car. Her hair was free of the hairnet and flying wildly in the wind. She pulled her coat tighter around her and folded her arms over her chest.

"It's late and I have to be up early tomorrow to help my grandma prepare for Thanksgiving dinner. I'm going to be knocked out as soon as my head hits the pillow."

"Do you have a lot of family coming?" We stopped in front of a black Toyota. Elodie clicked the button to unlock the car before tossing her things inside and turning back to me.

"My parents, my brother, and a few extended family members. My grandma likes to cook way too much food. So we'll be eating leftovers for the next two weeks." She rolled her eyes, but I could see the faint smile on her lips.

"It's usually just me and my immediate family, but my mom cooks enough to feed the entire neighborhood as well." I leaned against the hood of the car and studied her. It was getting late, and we should probably head home, but I didn't want to end the conversation.

"It's one of my favorite parts about the holidays; spending time with family. Everyone gathering under the same roof to spend time together before the responsibilities of everyday life steal our attention again." She let out a dreamy sigh. I smiled at her. Typically, my family got on my last nerve during the holiday season, but hearing her phrase it that way was nice. My family and I don't get together much during the year, but we always manage to spend time together during the super important days.

"Is family important to you?"

She chewed on her lip thoughtfully before responding. "Yes, it is. I know not everyone is as fortunate as I was to have a supportive family growing up, so I want to give back as much as I can."

"Is that why you volunteered tonight?" I asked, "To give them a sense of spending time with family?"

When her gaze focused on me again, my insides warmed. I rubbed my hands together, pretending to be cold, but really just needing something to distract myself from what her eyes were doing to me. After a moment of silence, she nodded before turning back to stare off into the empty parking lot.

"I never thought about it that way, but yes. I think it is."

"You strike me as someone who has a lot of love to give." I paused. "I'd like to experience that one day." My comment surprised us both. I had been thinking it but hadn't planned to say it. The look on her face when she whipped her head in my direction made me want to take it back immediately and apologize for overstepping, but instead, I held her gaze. She studied me for a moment, chewing on her bottom lip.

"I think I'd like that too."

Our conversation played repeatedly in my mind. Even though Principal Ardell had given me her number, I confirmed it with her before we left. Just to make sure she was okay with me having it.

She had promised to text me over this short break so we could discuss the musical even though that was the last thing on my mind.

Now, I sat in front of my television, staring blankly. An episode of Martin that I could quote from memory played on the screen. It was the Christmas episode from the fourth season when Martin was visited by three ghosts. The Scrooge reenactments were always my favorite Christmas stories because A Christmas Carol was my favorite classic. I made it a point to watch at least one version every year. My brother, Montrell would always complain that it was too predictable, but ever since we were children, we had seen every Scrooge reenactment that was out there. Even the random ones in a television series. I had turned this episode of Martin on as a distraction, but it wasn't working.

Was Elodie interested in me like I was interested in her? Or was she just being nice? I couldn't tell. She seemed to have a genuinely sweet spirit; I had seen the way she had interacted with the people we served at the shelter, but her kindness felt different when we talked. It felt like there could be interest there, but I didn't want to assume and ruin things before they could get started.

My phone buzzing in my pocket pulled my attention away from trying to read too much into an innocent conversation. My brows pulled together in surprise. I hadn't expected Jillian to be calling me. We don't talk very often.

"Hello?"

"Hey Mekhi, I am so sorry to interrupt your evening, but I'm desperate." Jillian sighed in my ear. I flicked off the television and glanced over at the clock. It was nearly two in the morning.

"Social work never sleeps. What's up?"

"I need your help."

Jillian Carmichael was a social worker turned friend I had met while I was still on the road. We had bonded at an event that I had been hired to play the piano for and have stayed connected ever since. She kept me in her back pocket as an emergency foster whenever her other plans fell through. Her calling me in the middle of the night right before a holiday could only mean one thing.

"You need a placement?" I asked, filling in the blanks myself before she could explain. I heard her deep sigh on the other end of the line, confirming that I was correct.

"Yes. He's a kid from your school. Kellan Washington. You know him?" Kellan was a student in my music class. He had the habit of being rambunctious, and slow to heed direction, but his infectious grin made it hard to stay angry at him for too long. He had a rare ear for music, but it was hidden beneath his antics.

"I do. What's his situation?" I asked, pulling myself from the couch, grateful for the distraction and sad that my plans for a lowkey night had now been ruined. I silently mourned the quiet night I had envisioned for myself as I prepared the guest room for his arrival.

"We had to remove him from the home. His current fosters have gotten caught up in illegal activity that I can't get into right now. I've been calling everywhere, but the homes are full, or they don't want to take on a new case right before the holiday."

"Give me twenty minutes to clean up and then bring him." I didn't hesitate. When I signed up to be an Emergency Foster, I knew this would be a possibility. Taking kids at a moment's notice for an undetermined period was a risk that came with it, but it was a risk that I was more than willing to take. Everyone deserves somewhere to go during the holidays.

When I heard the knock at my door a little over an hour later, I had just finished straightening up my home. As exhausted as I was, my nerves still buzzed with excitement. It'd been a while since I'd had a foster kid, and I was missing the company. This house can be so lonely with just me in it. I quickly put the broom back in the hall closet and opened the door. Jillian greeted me wearing a ratty sweatshirt and jeans. Behind her, looking just as exhausted as I felt, was Kellan holding a black trash bag. Gone was his usual smirk. Instead, he looked like he wanted nothing more than to crawl into bed and hide.

"Your bedroom is the first door on the left. Make yourself at home." I jerked my thumb over my shoulder. Without so much as a perfunctory glance in my direction, Kellan dragged the trash bag with him to the bedroom.

"You have no idea how grateful I am," Jillian whispered. "Are you sure this isn't too much trouble?"

I smiled at her. "Not at all. I know how it is."

"Thanksgiving is tomorrow and Jason and I had planned to-"

"Jillian," I interrupted, placing a hand on her shoulder, "It's fine. He can hang with me for the holidays. My family will love him."

"Thank you again."

"What can you tell me about his previous foster home? What should I be on the lookout for?" I asked.

"Kellan is a great kid. He tends to be a little withdrawn when he is first placed, but once he gets used to you, it'll be fine. His last social worker, Samantha, had too many cases on her workload and placed him in this situation without doing a thorough enough investigation of the home. She quit not too long ago, and we've been splitting the load between the rest of us," Jillian said, leaning against the door.

"I've had him in my music class and he seems to have a good ear, but he disrupts the class often," I replied, glancing back toward the guest room door. Jillian nodded, following my gaze.

"From what I have gathered in our interactions, he uses humor to deflect. Probably doesn't want anyone to figure out his situation. I know he loves music, though. He told me that your class is one of his favorites."

I smiled at that. I never knew whether I was getting through to them, so it was nice to hear that my lessons had some impact. Twelve was such a tricky age, being right there at the start of the teenage years, it could sometimes be hard for kids to settle into themselves. They had their likes and dislikes, but wanted to seem cool in front of their peers.

Kellan was a good kid, caught in an unfortunate situation. I knew it well. Years ago, I had been him. Using jokes and class disruptions to distract from the fact that I never knew where I would sleep from one night to the next. It's an experience that is easily taken for granted if you've never gone through it. Jillian and I talked for a few more minutes before her yawning took over, and she excused herself with promises to check in during the week. I sent a quick text to the family group chat to let them know that I'd be bringing an unexpected guest to dinner and then shuffled to my bedroom.

A quick peek into the guest room showed Kellan sprawled

out on the bed, not even under the covers, sound asleep. I pulled a blanket from the hall closet and placed it over him. It was an unfortunate situation to be pulled out of the home you had grown accustomed to right before the holidays started. Jillian had given me a brief rundown of the situation with his foster parents and while it wasn't ideal to be removed from the home this time of year, or even at all, I was happy he was no longer in that environment.

I wasn't sure how long I'd have him, but I knew how scary it was to be placed somewhere new at a moments notice, no matter what time of year it was. There had been so many nights where I laid awake in my new bed, in my new home, jumping at every single sound throughout the night. The exhaustion Kellan most likely felt from having to be on high alert so often was a feeling I had firsthand experience with. Fortunately, an absolutely amazing couple adopted my brother and me when I was a little older than Kellan, but before that day came, we had spent time in some horrible places.

While watching him for a few minutes, making sure he was okay, I decided to do whatever I could to ensure that while Kellan was with me, he could experience what it was like to be somewhere he could finally call home.

3

Mekhi

"I saw your text. How old is your new guest?" My mother's cheerful voice pulled me out of the groggy stupor I was in. My hopes of sleeping in were completely ruined. I knew I should have let it go to voicemail so I could sleep a little longer, but I had answered the phone without looking, still exhausted from work, the shelter, and Kellan's unexpected arrival.

"He's twelve, almost thirteen, I think." So much had happened in one night, I almost thought I had dreamed it. Jillian had texted me a few times to thank me again for helping and to give me a rundown on what to expect for the next few days. She was off until after Thanksgiving, but then she would work on finding placement for Kellan. Sounds of movement coming from the guest room told me I hadn't dreamed anything. I wanted to give Kellan enough space to adjust and decompress, but I knew he would probably be hungry soon. My own stomach rumbling was enough motivation to throw the covers off and get up. Even though my body protested the movement.

"We'll have more than enough food for him when you guys come. Does he have any allergies? What does he like to eat? Does he practice any specific religion?" I smiled at her, pelting me with excited questions. If there was anyone who cared more than me about fostering children, it was my mother. My brother and I were the two best things that happened to her. She told us this as often as she could from the moment we stepped into the home at thirteen and fifteen years old.

"I'm not sure yet, ma. I can send you the answers as I get them. Wanted to let him adjust to being here first before I gave him a questionnaire."

"Very funny. Alright, I'll let you two settle, but I expect answers to these questions before tomorrow. Do you hear me, Mekhi Amari? Don't wait until the last minute. I need time to prepare."

I laughed, "You mean you need time to send Dad out to get the stuff."

"Do what I said. You're not too old to get a beating. Remember that."

"Yes ma'am." My smile grew wider. She talked a tough game, but we both knew she didn't mean it. I appreciated her being so excited about making Kellan feel welcome. I knew my brother and my dad would be the same way. Dad especially. He never met a stranger, no matter where he went. Sometimes it was a bit embarrassing, but times like these I was grateful he was such a welcoming person. Kellan would probably need the extra welcome to really feel comfortable. I grabbed a shirt out of the closet and pulled it over my head as I opened the door to my bedroom. I stepped back in surprise to see Kellan standing there, with his small fist poised to knock. He flinched at the door opening so suddenly.

"Oh. Sorry." He mumbled, "You got any food?"

"Sure. What are you in the mood for?"

He tilted his head, studying me for a moment. "Can you cook?" His voice was skeptical and unbelieving. I made a show of glancing around the room like I was offended by his question.

"Look around. There's no one else here. How else would I eat? I've got cereal or I can make you something. I will warn you though, my Holiday French Toast can be addicting."

Kellan's eyes lit up. "I love French Toast."

He followed behind me as I headed towards the kitchen. He observed me as I pulled the ingredients out of the fridge and grabbed the loaf of brioche bread from the bread box. This was the most silent I had seen him since I started working at the school. He was always talking and laughing with someone around him. Seeing him so quiet, not so subtly looking around the apartment, was new.

I didn't want to push for conversation. I remembered from my time in new and unfamiliar homes, I always needed a second to gain my bearings before I could start talking. Something in the way his gaze kept flitting towards the living room set up and then back to me gave me the sense that he needed the same thing.

"You can go watch television if you want to." I offered. I grabbed a mixing bowl from the cabinet and put it next to the French Toast ingredients. Kellan watched me for a moment before retreating into the living room. Seconds passed before I saw his head pop back around the corner sheepishly.

"What's up?" I asked.

"Can I... help?" Kellan glanced down at his shoes. He looked embarrassed for asking.

"You can, but if you give away my secret ingredient, there will be dire consequences."

"What does dire mean?" Kellan reached for the loaf of bread.

"Wash your hands before you touch food." I flinched inwardly at how paternal I sounded. Kellan quickly dropped the bread and then turned to the sink apologetically. "Dire means terrible or dreadful. Okay, now pay attention. This is a serious recipe."

Kellan quickly got the hang of making French Toast after watching me make a couple slices. I felt confident enough to let him take over while I scrambled some eggs and made a few strips of bacon.

"You've got a text message," Kellan said, glancing down at the phone that I had discarded on the counter before we began cooking. I wiped my hands on the dishtowel and then tapped the screen, expecting to see a text from my mother fussing at me for not sending her a list of Kellan's favorite things. Instead, it was a message from Elodie. Seeing her name on my screen made my heart thump nervously in my chest.

I picked it up slowly, fighting to keep my excitement from showing in front of Kellan, and unlocked it. When we had confirmed our phone numbers before we left last night, she told me she would text me today. In the flurry of excitement that followed, I had almost forgotten she had made that promise.

Morning! Are you as exhausted as I am? I fell asleep as soon as I got home.

I smiled. So much has happened since we talked. I wondered if I should fill her in on everything that had transpired since leaving the homeless shelter. For some reason, I felt the urge to divulge everything to her.

I am, but for different reasons. I had an emergency foster placed with me last night.

Typing bubbles popped up immediately. I could only imagine what she was thinking.

Emergency foster? You're a foster parent? Wow! I have so many questions. How old is the kid? Girl or boy?

I reached for my plate, intending to take it with me to the living room to eat like I would if I were by myself, but thought against it. Instead, I made a beeline for the dining room, motioning for Kellan to follow me. He picked up his plate and shuffled after me, silently.

Boy. 12, I think. Maybe 13. I think he's actually in your class. Kellan?

The typing bubbles stopped. I briefly wondered if I had said too much. Maybe I shouldn't have shared that with her. Kellan took a bite of his French Toast and closed his eyes. I laughed at his reaction.

"I told you. Addicting." I grinned, taking a bite of my own

food. It had been a while since I'd made French Toast, but it was clear I hadn't lost my touch. It was a recipe that I'd picked up from my mom before I left for college. During my first year at the university, it was the only thing I knew how to make, and I survived on it for an embarrassing amount of time before I eventually learned how to cook other dishes. I'd had plenty of time to perfect the recipe.

My phone buzzed on the table, signifying another text. I shoved another forkful of food in my mouth and picked it up with my free hand. Kellan ignored me, hungrily shoveling food in his mouth. I couldn't be sure he was actually chewing before he swallowed the mouthful and reached for another. It made me wonder when the last time he'd had anything substantial to eat.

Hmm. Looks like I'm not the only one with a lot of love to give.

Her message made me pause, replaying the last bit of our conversation from last night. I hadn't meant to come on so strong, but something about her drew me in before I realized what was happening. The way she had looked at me still made me shudder with excitement. It had been a while since anyone had been able to pique my interest this much. My last girlfriend and I had split years ago. Right before I had taken my first job on the road. I wanted to explore my music, while she wanted to explore other men. I'd found out she was texting other guys and broke it off right before I left.

I'd expected to feel some type of sadness about it since we had been together for so long, but I kept going as if she and I had never met. It made me realize the relationship had been heading nowhere anyway and even if I hadn't had the excuse of leaving for my career, we probably would have fizzled out, eventually. Since her, I haven't been able to connect with anyone in a way that left a lasting impression. Until now. Until Elodie.

Being next to her last night, serving people at the shelter, was more of an enjoyable experience than I had expected. It was the most fun I'd had during one of those shifts. Her energy was so easy and fun. I found myself wanting to impress her somehow. Our first practice for the musical wasn't until after the Thanksgiving break ended, but maybe we should get together before then. We needed to decide what songs to sing before we presented them to the kids to learn right?

I picked up my phone again and opened Apple Pay. I sent her a few dollars to get a coffee. I hoped she wouldn't be offended by my gesture. To make sure it couldn't be misinterpreted, I sent a follow-up text.

Grab coffee, my treat. Consider it an early thank you for helping with this musical. Happy Thanksgiving!

"Mr. Davis?" Kellan asked after a moment of silence had passed. I had been so wrapped up in my thoughts and texting Elodie, I hadn't realized I'd been quiet for a while. I looked up to see Kellan's plate almost empty and his face somber.

"Yes?" I almost didn't hear what him, but the sudden seriousness in his tone made me stop and look at him. He was staring down at his hands, still covered in powdered sugar and cinnamon.

"With tomorrow being Thanksgiving and all, you can leave me here. I won't mind."

I was too stunned to respond right away. Kellan's gaze stayed fixed on his fingers. His shoulders hunched forward in embarrassment. He looked like he was trying to shrink himself as much as possible. I waited, hoping he would look up, but he didn't.

"Kellan," I began, unsure of what to say. "Why would you think you'd need to stay here alone?"

"Thanksgiving is for families. I'm not a part of the family." He shrugged. There was a gruffness to his voice that wasn't there before. "It's cool. I don't care."

"While you're here, you're a part of the family."

His head shot up in surprise. I raised an eyebrow at him, trying not to show the sadness I felt. For that to be his immediate reaction to being included, then he was most likely used to being overlooked. That was something I unfortunately understood. It was a common occurrence in homes with foster children some people did not deserve to have.

"Really? But-"

"But nothing," I interrupted firmly. "Thanksgiving is for everyone. You'll be there." Kellan fell silent. The room felt tense and heavy, full of unspoken emotion. I wanted to comfort him, but I didn't want to do too much too soon. Kellan swallowed, before clearing his throat quickly and nodding.

"Okay."

We finished our meal in silence. My phone buzzed on the table. Messages from the family group chat. It was most likely my mother, demanding to know the answers to her questions.

"There is a very angry woman on the other end of this phone who demands to know your favorite dessert and favorite side dish." I sighed, after skimming over the many text messages in the group chat. My brother had only responded a few times, but most of the messages were from my mom trying her hardest to threaten me into providing the answers she was sought after. Kellan's eyes widened.

"I like cheesecake." He put a finger to his chin in mock contemplation, "And mac and cheese!"

"A man of good taste. I dig it." I typed a quick response before placing my phone back down on the table. "We've got time before we need to head out. What would you like to do?"

"I saw a piano in your other room."

I raised an eyebrow. "When did you have time to snoop?"

"You were sleeping for a long time."

I shook my head. I didn't think I'd been sleeping all that long, but when you no longer have the energy of a twelve-year-old kid, your turnaround time is more extended. I glanced around at the disaster in the kitchen. Dirty dishes littered the counter and little piles of powdered sugar were all over the floor. The bacon wrapper and the eggshells sat near the garbage, but not quite in it. Cooking was always messy work, but it seemed like this time was messier than usual.

"Well, we need to clean up this kitchen before we do any else."

Kellan wrinkled his nose at me as if I had asked him to do something outrageous. "You clean?"

"Again. Look around. Do you see anyone else here but me?"

"You don't have a maid for that?"

"On a teacher's salary?" I scoffed, "Please. You can sweep, or you can wash dishes. Your pick."

"Will you teach me a Christmas song on the piano when we're done?"

I wanted to smile. I loved it when someone showed interest in music, especially piano. I wanted to jump at the opportunity to teach them something. I remembered Jillian mentioning that Kellan did well with music. He would do well in class, but was usually too distracted by his classmates to progress in the way he should. A solo lesson would give me the chance to see where his skills were.

"It depends on how well you clean. Hop to it." Kellan jumped out of his chair excitedly, grabbing the empty plates to take them to the kitchen. I chuckled at his enthusiasm and grabbed the broom out of the hall closet. So far, so good. It was his first few hours here with me, so I couldn't expect too much just yet, but he was adjusting better than I thought he would.

I made a mental note to update Jillian when we had made it through an entire day. I was excited to see how he would fit in with my family. I already knew my mother would love him. Probably too much. She would end up getting attached before he left. I could guarantee it, but she knew how these things worked.

As I watched his poor attempt at sweeping the kitchen, I couldn't help but be grateful he had landed with me and not with someone else who wouldn't necessarily want him around. So many good kids have been ruined by a system that doesn't care about them. If it hadn't been for my parents, my brother and I would have been included in that number.

Kellan had a good head on his shoulders. He would most likely do fine wherever he ended up, but I couldn't help but hope he'd get the same luck as I did.

4

Elodie

Mekhi and I ended up promising to text each other after we left the homeless shelter last night and I had been obsessing ever since, wondering if I should text him first or wait until he texted me. Our conversation inspired me to write. I had gone home and fallen asleep, but then woke up a little later to put words on paper. I worried if I slept on the inspiration for too long, I'd lose that spark. By the time I looked up from my computer, it was well into the morning. I had closed my laptop and slid back into the bed hoping to grab several hours of sleep before I was due at my grandmother's house to help begin preparation for Thanksgiving dinner, but of course, that hope was crushed immediately when she began calling me at eight o'clock sharp.

Now I stood in front of my mirror, exhaustion weighing heavily on my entire body. I had no regrets, though. I'd written more in those few hours than I'd been able to in months. When writer's block had been sitting there like the devil on my shoulder for so long, I knew better than to ignore inspiration. Even if it struck at the worst possible time.

By the time I dragged myself to my car, I was debating asking the girls if we could reschedule the book club meeting tonight, but if I missed tonight, who knew when I would be able to see my girls next? I'd just have to get some coffee and power through. I glanced at my phone as I was getting in the car, hoping there would be a text from Mekhi. There wasn't. Before I could talk myself out of it, I sent a quick message to him. No use waiting around when I could make a move myself.

He responded within seconds, making me smile. It felt good having someone I was into express interest in me. I read his message about my student Kellan being placed temporarily with him, surprised by the information. I'd had no idea that Mekhi was a foster parent. The thought sent a warm fuzzy feeling through my body. We had talked for a good while outside of the homeless shelter last night, but that had never come up. The conversation felt so natural that I had almost forgotten there was still so much we needed to learn about each other.

I quickly logged into my bank account to see if I could swing for gas and a large coffee. There were still two weeks left until payday, but if I pinched pennies as hard as I could, maybe I could stretch it enough for the splurge. I deflated at the minuscule balance waiting for me. There was enough for coffee, but not much else.

I would have to get gas and just hope that my grandmother had decent coffee waiting at the house. The chances of that were extremely low. She usually opts for the cheap stuff no matter how hard we try to convince her that other brands are better. My phone vibrated again. I glanced down at my watch, thinking it was a text from one of my girls or Alex, and froze. It was an Apple Pay notification from Mekhi for fifteen dollars.

I stared at my phone screen in shock for a moment, unsure of what to do or how to feel. This was so needed and so unexpected. It gave me goosebumps. The mention of my tiredness made him spring into action with a kind gesture that was small in the grand scheme of things but meant so much in the moment.

Thank you.

My response felt almost dry, but I wasn't sure what else to say without sounding like I was reading way too much into the situation. I put my phone away and concentrated on the drive to my Grandmother Amada's house. If I let myself obsess over the potential meaning of Mehki being so nice, I'd get nothing done and there was way too much to do today to get distracted.

By the time I'd made it to her house, venti cold brew in hand, I felt a little less tired. Maybe it was my second wind, or maybe it was the coffee coursing through my bloodstream. Either way, I was able to perk up in enough time. As I pulled into the driveway at my Grandmother Amada, or Grandmada's as I lovingly called her, house I spotted her moving around the kitchen through the window. I groaned inwardly; she was already working, which meant there wouldn't be much time to talk and chit-chat. She would expect me to come in and hit the ground running.

"Hey Grandmada!" I called, as I unlocked her front door with my key. When I entered the kitchen, she was on her hands and knees looking for something in the lower cabinets. For someone in their late seventies, my grandmother moved around with ease. Her slate gray curls were braided straight back, and her muumuu hung loosely around her body. A thin sheen of sweat coated her umber skin.

"Hey sweet baby," she kissed me on the cheek. "You look tired. You been sleeping?"

"I was up late last night working on my novel. I was finally able to connect the dots in the storyline like I wanted." My grandmother was the one person who truly understood my love for writing. She had several novels under her belt before she decided to focus on raising her family.

"How did you figure it out?" she asked, grabbing the ingredients to make her homemade macaroni and cheese. I chewed on my bottom lip, debating whether to tell her how I figured it all out.

"A friend of mine inspired me during our conversation after my shift at the homeless shelter. He-"

"He?" she interrupted; her full attention now fixed on my face. I could feel the heat rising in my cheeks.

"Yes. His name is Mekhi Davis. He's the new music teacher at my job. He was at the shelter serving with me last night. We ended up talking and getting to know each other a little bit. We're going to be working on the musical together at the school. He even bought me this coffee as a thank you for being willing to help." I lifted my half-empty coffee cup.

"Hmm." She replied. Her eyes narrowed as she looked at me for a moment. "I guess it's time then."

I watched, confused, as she shuffled out of the kitchen. I could hear her rifling around in her bedroom before she reappeared holding a rectangular box. It was a bit early to exchange gifts. A mild flash of panic hit me. I hadn't even started shopping for Christmas gifts yet. I had nothing to offer.

"Here. I want you to open this." She said, sliding the box towards me. I took one final swig of my coffee and wiped my damp fingers on my pants before reaching for the box. I had no idea what was in it, but this felt like a monumental moment. The vibe of the room shifted into a more serious note.

"What is it?" I was already pulling it open before she could respond. Inside lay a gorgeous leather-bound journal and a delicate feather pen. It looked like it would fall apart if not handled with the utmost care. The more I studied the journal and pen, the more I realized I had seen it before as a kid, tucked away under her clothes in her bottom drawer. Why was she giving me her old journal? I had planned to spend hard earned money that I couldn't really spare to get her a one-of-a-kind pearl necklace for Christmas.

There's still time to find something else, I thought, trying to school my features into a grateful smile. She saw right through my act and shook her head, a small smile on her lips. She gingerly pulled the journal out of the box and placed her hand on top. The lilac nail polish on her perfectly manicured fingers glittered brightly.

"My grandmother gave me this notebook and pen when I was just a few years younger than you," she began. "It's special."

I tilted my head, trying to find what was so special about this plain notebook and pen. It was pretty; it looked like it had been expensive back in the day, but I couldn't see what made it different than any others made with the same materials.

"What makes it special?"

"It brought your grandfather to me."

I snickered. We both knew she met my grandfather at the grocery store, struggling to choose between two brands of toilet paper. This was a story they had drilled into my head over and over as a child. I knew it so well; it felt like I lived it. What did a journal have to do with that? I continued to laugh, expecting her to laugh with me at the obvious joke, but her expression remained serious. The laughter died in my throat.

"Grandmada, what do you mean this journal brought Grandpop to you? You guys met in the store, remember?" My eyebrows furrowed with concern. Was she losing her memory? Is that what this was? She huffed and folded her arms across her chest.

"I'm not crazy, Elodie. Stop looking at me like I've grown an extra head."

"Sorry, I'm just-"

She held up a hand to stop me. My mouth clamped shut out of habit. Growing up, when she held up that hand, it meant stop talking before it pops you in the mouth. Even as an adult, I knew not to test her. My grandmother motioned for me to sit on the stool nearest her.

"We met in the grocery store," she began. "That was after my grandmother gave me this journal and told me it would bring me to the love of my life." I waited, expecting her to burst into laughter at any moment. She held my gaze without a trace of humor in her expression.

"Isn't that just a coincidence?"

"No, child. It was not. The journal and this pen work together to create magic. It will write the beginning of your story, but it is up to you to let the story take root."

I reached for the journal and the pen skeptically, while she watched my movements. I put the pen to the paper, attempting to write my name on one of the empty pages. Nothing happened. The pen had no ink.

"How am I supposed to write anything if there's no ink?" I complained, shaking the pen in frustration. My grandmother grabbed my wrist gently and removed the pen from my grip.

"You do not write the story. The journal writes the story. You, my dear granddaughter, must live it."

"So, she gave you this journal and told you it was magic?"

Later that night, I was sitting with my best friends: Deja, Audrey, and Monae in our favorite bookshop in town while we waited for Brina to show up. It was our book club meeting, but I'd spent the majority of the opening minutes venting about my grandmother and her magical journal from earlier this morning.

The bookstore was quiet. Most people were bustling around getting ready for the holiday. Even though all of us had families and other plans for Thanksgiving, we squeezed in this time for each other. I truly treasured these moments with the group of women I had met during a pivotal time in my life. It's rare you stay close with college friends once everyone graduates, but I was fortunate enough that we held on to each other, even as we all ventured into our own careers and lives as adults.

Deja raised her perfectly waxed eyebrow, trying and failing to hide her smirk. All of them listened while I tried my best to repeat the information my grandmother had given me about the journal. Saying it made me feel just as loopy as she sounded when she was telling me to trust in the journal's magic. I sighed and ran a hand over my curls.

I'd tried my best to seem like I was receptive to what my grandmother was telling me, but it was hard to overlook the fact that it made no sense. No matter how many times she tried to explain it to me, I couldn't wrap my head around any of it. A magical journal that is supposed to point me in the direction of my one true love. I didn't even want true love. At least not right now. I was too busy trying to get this novel off the ground and hoping for a salary increase at work.

Monae reached over and grabbed the zucchini fries Audrey had brought with her. I hadn't had the chance to ask her to bring the Philly cheese roll-ups, but I wasn't too hurt. The fries weren't that bad. The journal and pen sat on the table in the middle of our circle, taunting me.

"She could have given me a gift card or something. What's

wrong with a target card? I don't need magic. I need money." I grumbled. I didn't want to seem ungrateful, but I had plenty of journals and notebooks. I didn't need another one.

Audrey reached out and patted my knee. "She obviously wanted you to have it for a reason. Just be patient."

I rolled my eyes. Audrey was always the sensible one. Back in college, when we would be delirious with stress about classes and trying to juggle our social lives, Audrey stayed levelheaded and mature. I could count on one hand how many times I saw her lose her cool. She remained unshakeable even in the craziest moments. When she opened her restaurant with no type of business experience and no idea where to start, she barely broke a sweat. The only times I saw her cry was when her father passed, and when she was forced to repeat a year in culinary school for reasons, she wouldn't share with the rest of us.

Most of the time it was an admirable quality, but sometimes, I just wanted her to join in on my frustration. I reached out to grab another zucchini fry, unsure of how to respond. Deja gingerly picked up the journal using only two of her fingers. She held it out in front of her as if it were dirty. I watched as she inspected it, turning her wrist left and right to see if she spotted anything of note.

"It looks like a regular journal to me." She said, scrunching her nose.

"Yes." I grabbed the journal from her and placed it beside me. "But she claims it's magic. I don't know. Maybe it'll show me something."

"Maybe it can show me some good di-"

"I'm so sorry I'm late!" Brina came bursting into the bookshop, cutting off the end of Deja's sentence. Brina practically tumbled over to the table, a human tornado in a perfectly tailored pinstripe suit. "Court went longer than I planned, and it pushed my entire day behind."

She huffed and pulled at the hair tie holding her long braids up in a bun on the top of her head. I watched as they tumbled freely down her shoulders, the telltale sign she was officially done with work for the day. I handed her the tray of zucchini fries and laughed as her face wrinkled in confusion.

"Is this healthy food? No thank you, I prefer my fries to be greasy and made with potatoes. Catch me up. What did I miss?"

She listened intently as I filled her in on the visit with my grandmother and the magical journal. I expected her to laugh or hint at disbelief like the rest of them had, but instead, she shrugged and swiped up the drink menu from the coffee shop attached to the bookstore, off the table.

"Stranger things have happened. I think we're all a bit overdue for a Christmas miracle."

"Speaking of Christmas. My principal at work signed me up to work with Mekhi, the new music teacher, for the school play this year."

All four girls perked up.

"Mekhi? That sounds like a brother. He black?" Deja asked, leaning forward in her seat. Her purple and black faux locs spilled over her shoulder. I nodded, trying to suppress a smile.

"He is. My principal gave me his number last night, but then he ended up showing up at the homeless shelter. We had a really good time. The vibe was noticeable." I could feel the heat rising in my cheeks as all four of them stared at me. Truth is, I had been thinking about Mekhi off and on all day.

"Oh? Sounds like that journal is working its magic already." Brina giggled, wriggling her eyebrows at me. I rolled my eyes at her. It was definitely a coincidence.

My girls and I spent the next few hours laughing and catching up. The book we were supposed to be discussing was JL Seegar's new release Revive Me, but the majority of our book club meeting was spent taking turns giving each other a rundown of what had been happening in our lives since our last meeting.

We normally keep each other updated throughout the weeks in the group chat, but sometimes that just wasn't enough. I explained the plot of my novel to all of them, including the newer parts that I had just recently figured out, while they hung on my every word.

By the time I had finally made it home that night, the coffee and the excitement of the day had worn off. Leaving me absolutely bone tired. I barely put my bonnet on before I was sinking into my blankets, determined to get a solid night's sleep.

Before I could close my eyes and let sleep take over, a weird feeling hit me. I sat up, turned on the light, and looked around the room. There was no one here aside from my dog, Bark Twain, curled up in a little fuzzy black ball at the foot of my bed. My gaze drifted to my desk, where the journal that I could have sworn I'd left closed was now open. The pen moved back and forth furiously.

I watched, confused and a little scared. Was I dreaming or was there a ghost? It's too early in the holiday season to be visited by the Ghost of Christmas Past, present, or future, plus I hadn't been acting like Scrooge. So why was I looking at this happening? More importantly... how?

I threw the covers back and stepped gingerly out of the bed. Bark Twain lifted his head, his ears flopping to one side as he watched me inching towards my desk like a madwoman. The pen flew across the pages as if someone was scribbling as quickly as they could.

When I reached my desk, the pen had gone still, resting against the notebook as if it hadn't just been racing across the pages. I picked up the journal gently, so I could read what had been written. My hands shook nervously. In deep, loopy, cursive, there was an entry.

Dear Diary

Recently Elodie interacted with the man who would have a great impact on her life They had spent so much time in the same school but hadn t had the chance to speak until they both worked at the homeless shelter Conversation was easy between them making it feel like they had been friends forever Both were excited to work on the musical together They re meeting just in time to begin their love story Let us watch as it unfolds

5

Elodie

The next morning, I couldn't even focus on it being Thanksgiving. All I could think about was the magical hoodoo voodoo this journal on my desk conjured up the night before. I had taken a picture of the entry and sent it to the group chat, hoping they could offer any kind of explanation to clear my head.

So far, Deja was the only one who answered just long enough to accuse me of writing the message in the journal myself and make jokes at my expense. I paused, trying to remember if I had somehow done it while sleepwalking, but pushed away the thought. I know what I saw, even if I couldn't make enough sense of it to explain it to someone else.

I took a shower and got ready to head to my grandmother's house. Despite the weird situation with the journal, I was excited to spend time with my family. It had been a while since we were all under the same roof. The gentle Christmas music playing while I got ready made me think about Mekhi. I didn't want to text him while he had so much going on, but I wanted to check in and see how he and Kellan were doing. The idea of Mekhi being a foster dad stirred something in me. As a teacher, you had to have at least a slight passion for helping children, but to take on a foster required a different level of dedication.

I hummed along to the music while I styled my hair in two space buns with loose tendrils framing my face. It was the perfect hairstyle to go with my burnt orange sweats and black fitted top. Cute Thanksgiving turkey earrings gave it the finishing touch of holiday spirit without doing too much. I'd save the more obnoxious festive outfits for December. Since there wasn't much Thanksgiving attire to choose from, other than dressing up like a pilgrim or an Indian, I usually cracked open the Christmas wardrobe as soon as Halloween ended. My earring and sweater collection was big enough to wear something different every day, if I really put thought into it. Holiday fashion was something I took seriously, even though my friends and family would sometimes poke fun at my outfit choices. It was all a part of the tradition.

"Elodie!" a deep voice boomed from my living room, followed by footsteps. I let out a groan.

"You're only supposed to use your key for emergencies, Javon!" I yelled back, rolling my eyes. My little brother peeked around the door frame with a mischievous glint in his eyes, his black and honey blonde locs falling freely around his face.

"This is an emergency. You know grandma will have our heads if we aren't there on time."

We were required to arrive at Grandmada's house at eleven am sharp, which meant we needed to be pulling up to the house and walking up the driveway by ten fifty or we would never hear the end of it.

"I'm not worried about that." I glanced down at my watch, to be sure. We had enough time. Javon smirked at me and flopped backwards on my bed. I turned, ready to fuss at him for sitting on my clean sheets in his outside clothes, then thought against it. "How are you?"

"I'm fine." He replied quickly. Too quickly. I narrowed my eyes. He held my gaze for a minute before he cracked under the pressure and sighed. "I'm not as great as I could be, but I'm getting there."

Javon and his long-time boyfriend had recently separated and as much as he tried to act like it didn't phase him, I knew my brother. Underneath the charming smile and the lighthearted jokes, I knew he was badly hurting. I nodded. As much as I wanted him to open up to me completely about how he was feeling, that answer was as good as I was going to get. Javon had never been one to openly express his pain.

While he mindlessly scrolled on his phone, I finished getting ready. My eyes kept drifting back to the journal on my desk. It was still closed from where I had slammed it shut earlier in a panic, but curiosity was getting the better of me.

"Von, can I ask you a question?"

He barely glanced up from his phone. "Yes, those earrings do look ridiculous."

"They're adorable, first of all. But no. I'm serious." I threw a nearby pillow at him. "Do you believe in magic?"

The look he gave me would have been hilarious if I wasn't completely serious. He stared at me as if waiting for me to laugh or admit that I was joking. When I didn't, he put his phone down and sat up.

"Where is this question coming from?"

"Grandmada gave me a journal last night. She told me it was magic," I began slowly, "And it was going to write my love story if I believed in it. Which I thought was a joke at first, but then last night I saw it."

"Saw what, exactly?"

"The notebook. It was on my desk and somehow it had fallen open and the pen was just flying across the pages like someone was scribbling as fast as they could." All the words came tumbling out of my mouth in a tangled mess. Javon stared at me for a split second before he burst out laughing. A full-on shoulder shaking guffaw that had him falling back on the bed and clutching his stomach. Embarrassment heated my cheeks.

"Sis, what have you been smoking? Please share." He wheezed, slapping a hand over his mouth. His cerulean blue nails popped against his skin. I could barely get a word out before he started laughing again.

"Never mind. Just forget I asked." I mumbled, grabbing my purse and my keys, "Let's go."

Javon peeled himself off my bed, still chuckling as we walked out to my car. I never should have said anything to him about it. I had been hoping he would be more open to hearing what I was saying instead of dismissing me completely, but he clearly wasn't. I wasn't even sure if I was in the space to accept it when I had seen it with my own eyes.

By the time we made it to Grandmada's house, we had two minutes to spare. Our parents' car was already in the driveway next to her old school Buick that had seen better days, but she refused to part with. Other family members' vehicles dotted the large driveway as well. When we burst through the door, everyone turned to look at us.

"Hey, you two." My mother said, with a slight smirk on her face. She knew firsthand how strict her mother was about punctuality around dinner, especially Thanksgiving. She knew that Javon and I had to be burning rubber to get here. Grandmada wasn't like the typical family that announced dinner would be ready by two, but you didn't sit down to eat until almost six o'clock. If she said dinner would be ready by two, don't even think about arriving late.

"Hey Mom. Hi Daddy." I greeted both of my parents before slipping my arm around Grandmada's shoulders. "The woman of the hour!"

She rolled her eyes at my comment, but slipped her arm around my waist to return the embrace. When our eyes met, there was a knowing glint in her expression. I quickly glanced away, not wanting to have that conversation in front of everyone. The last thing I wanted to do was cause everyone to laugh at me the same way Javon did. I don't think my ego could take it.

When we finished eating, my stomach was so full it felt like it would pop out of my sweatpants. This was exactly why I didn't wear regular pants. Anyone who has had my grandmother's cooking knows to come comfortably dressed because you will be stuffing your face. Javon and our dad went into the living room with the rest of our male family members. Minutes later, you could hear their cheering for the football teams throughout the house.

My mother and I pulled the Christmas decorations out from the attic and began sorting through them. Each year, after Thanksgiving dinner, we would go through the Christmas decorations to make sure all the lights worked and none of the ornaments had gotten broken during the year. I was trying to untangle myself from a string of lights when Grandmada motioned for me to follow her. I picked up the pile of lights and followed her down the hall to her bedroom.

"So?" she asked, closing the door behind her.

I raised an eyebrow. "So what?"

"You know what I'm asking about, child. The journal! Did the process begin?"

I hesitated, unsure of how much I wanted to share. She waited, arms folded across her chest and eyebrow raised as if she already knew the answer. The clock above her dresser ticked loudly in the silence. The longer I stayed silent, the more her eyes narrowed. There was no use lying about it.

"Yes. As I was getting ready to fall asleep, it flipped open, and the pen started writing. It was terrifying, I mean-"

"Oh, wonderful!" She interrupted, clapping her hands excitedly. I stopped mid-sentence, confused.

"Wonderful? I'm telling you, a ghost snuck into my house last night to write a weird journal entry, and you're telling me this is a good thing?"

"It wasn't a ghost, Elodie. It's the journal. I told you it would write the love story if you let it." I stared at her in disbelief. I almost wanted to laugh like Javon did, but I didn't want to hurt her feelings. The entire thing made no sense.

"I'm not even thinking about love right now, Grandmada!" I protested, "I'm literally just trying to write and maybe travel at some point, if my job will let me take enough time off."

"Nonsense, girl. All those love stories you read and you watch on television. All of those stories you write about the knight in shining armor that comes to save the day. You are more of a romantic than you give yourself credit for." She placed her hands on my shoulders. My body sagged a little under her touch, as if her hands were weights that were pulling me down.

"But... I have nothing to offer."

"Enough of that foolishness. You have so much to offer and any man-" she glanced around and lowered her voice to a whisper, "or woman... would be lucky to have you."

I threw my head back and laughed, "How very progressive of you."

"I am the epitome of progress. Now, don't close yourself off to experiencing love just because you aren't where you think you should be. Allow yourself to enjoy the moment."

Her words caught me off guard. I opened my mouth to respond when my phone buzzed. I pulled it out of my pocket, wondering who could be texting me. My girls were all with their families or celebrating the holidays in their own ways. I clicked the side button on my phone to see Mekhi's name flash across the screen. I smiled to myself.

I was thinking we should probably meet up before Monday so we can discuss what songs we want to do for this musical.

Did I want to see Mekhi before school started again? Honestly, I did. Something about him made me want to be near him as much as I could. Our conversations were so natural and full of ease. I wanted more of them.

That's probably a good idea. What did you have in mind?

It'd need to be something kid friendly; I don't want to leave Kellan alone for too long.

I was so busy typing out my response that when my grandmother cleared her throat, I jumped, completely forgetting we had just been talking. When she met my gaze, her eyes twinkled.

"Seems like you're enjoying the moment already." She quipped, a smile pulling at her lips. I could feel my cheeks heating again. I didn't want to be that giggly girl who jumped every time the phone rang with a text or call from her man, who wasn't really her man. But as I stood here, practically giddy just because his name popped up on my phone, I felt like I had already lost that battle.

"We're just friends," I replied half-heartedly. She nodded, not believing me for a second. "He probably doesn't even feel the same way."

"Alright, sweet girl." She patted my cheek and then left the room, leaving me to wonder if I was thinking too far ahead too soon. The fact that the journal entry had been about him made me excited to see where things went, but I didn't want to sabotage myself by pushing for too much before we were ready. How do you explain to someone that you're so enthusiastic about seeing the relationship progress because of an allegedly magical journal without sounding like you need to be committed?

I can come to your place.

I sent the message before I could talk myself out of it. The dreaded three bubbles popped up and then disappeared. I watched, anxiety growing stronger in my chest as Mekhi kept typing and deleting his message.

Before he could respond, and dig the embarrassment in even deeper, I hurriedly sent a follow-up message. One that would hopefully explain what I meant without making it sound like I was trying to cross a boundary.

Kellan probably still needs a second to chill. If I come to you, he can relax in his room or whatever.

I held my breath after pressing send, praying to whoever would listen that he didn't think I was trying to come on to him. There was a pause before the bubbles popped up again. When his response came through, I held the phone away from my face and tried my best to read it by squinting. Terrified that if I looked at it straight on, the embarrassment would swallow me whole.

Okay, cool. I have a piano here that we could use.

I breathed a sigh of relief. He didn't think too much of my suggestion, which is good. I locked my phone and went to put it in my pocket when the realization of what I just agreed to settled in. I'm going to his house. We may have worked together and had a pleasant time at the homeless shelter together, but overall, I didn't know much about him. What if he was a creep? I chewed on my bottom lip nervously. He probably wouldn't have been trusted to be an emergency foster if he was a creep, but still, the possibility is there.

Just because the journal seemed to be a fan of his and we'd had a few decent conversations, doesn't mean I should throw all common sense out the window, does it? My mind drifted back to what Grandmada had just said to me before she left the room. I needed to enjoy the moment.

"Elodie! Where are those Christmas lights?!" My mother's impatient voice carried from the hallway. Who knows how long I had actually been standing here turning over this situation in my head. I hurriedly reached for the lights that had somehow gotten re-tangled since I entered this bedroom and tried to make at least a little progress on the mess. The more I pulled, the messier they became. I let out a huff of frustration. This was a two-man job. Still wasn't sure how they became this tangled every year between taking them off the tree and putting them back in the box. I was the one that took them down last year and I had put them up in such a way as to not have this problem again.

"Elodie!!" my mother called again. Her tone indicated I had a few seconds to make an appearance before she came looking for me herself.

"Coming! Sorry!" I called. Defeated, I picked up the lights and hurried out of the room.

Later that night, stuffed full of food and desperate for some rest, I crawled into my bed. Bark Twain snuggled next to me with a quick wag of his tail. I patted him on the head and tugged my bonnet down tighter before slipping further under the covers.

I'd just reached that delirious state between awake and asleep when I heard a loud rustling. My eyes shot open, looking around the room for the sound. Bark Twain's ears perked, letting me know he was hearing the same thing I was. I searched the dark bedroom until my eyes fell on the journal sitting on my nightstand where

I had left it that morning. The pages were flipping wildly until it landed on an empty page. The pen that lay next to the journal lifted and began scribbling hastily. Mildly annoyed, I watched the pen move. Was there not an option to have it do its thing during the day? Why was it always interrupting me mid-sleep?

I waited until the scribbling stopped before getting out of the bed and cautiously approaching the journal, curious to know what it would say this time. The writing swirled and looped across the page, writing about something that hadn't happened yet.

Dear Diary

Elodie visited Mekhi s home for the very first time It felt strange walking into his world and seeing more of who he was but it also felt right Like she was finally coming home after a long and aimless journey

Kellan his new foster and one of her loudest students was there too Seeing him in Mekhi s space quiet shy yet still full of energy made her see him in a new light He wasn t the difficult student she d always thought him to be He was just a kid trying to find his place When he watched with rapt fascination while Mekhi played the songs she realized how much he must be soaking in even if he doesn t show it Mekhi s gentle patience with him was something Elodie hadn t expected She caught glimpses of the bond they were starting to form and it warmed her heart

They spent the evening practicing for the musical; the

piano filling the room with sweet Christmas music
creating a comfortable rhythm between them. It was
that exact moment they both began to feel like they
were a part of something deeper than just a rehearsal
Something real

6

Mekhi

"Can I have another piece of cheesecake?" Kellan asked. My mother beamed as she sliced into what was left of the strawberry cheesecake, most of which he had single-handedly consumed on his own. I smiled at the two of them as they chattered happily like they had known each other for years. I had no doubt my family would embrace him, but it was comforting to see how well he fit in. I got up and headed into the living room, fighting the sleep that hits after a heavy meal. My stomach was full to the point of being uncomfortable, but I didn't regret one bite of anything. The entire meal was delicious.

I wanted to give myself a chance to let my food settle before I began packing up the leftovers that I planned to survive on for the next week. One of the best things about Thanksgiving was the leftovers. If you played your cards correctly, you wouldn't have to worry about figuring out what to eat for a while. I made a mental note to take some of the extra cheesecake I know my mother had hiding in the back of the refrigerator.

"How long will Kellan be staying with you?" My brother Montrell sat down on the couch next to me and plucked the remote from my hands. I watched with dwindling interest as he flipped through the channels for something else to watch. He landed on the football game. I was more of a basketball man myself, but my father and Montrell both liked to sit in front of the television and yell at football teams. Growing up, you could hear the two of them stomping throughout the house whenever there was an exciting game on.

"I'm not sure. I'll have to check with Jillian and see what she says. She's working on a placement for him after Thanksgiving." My gaze drifted to my phone in my hand, debating on whether or not I should text Elodie to see how she was doing, maybe invite her out before school starts back and we have to focus on the musical.

"Are you still looking to go back on the road soon?"

I had mentioned to Montrell before that I had planned to go back on the road at the top of the year. It was still the plan at some point, but with recent events, who knows where I'll be at the beginning of the year.

"I might be. Still thinking about it. Why? You gonna miss me?" I grinned.

Montrell made a disgusted face. "Not a chance." His phone chiming in his pocket momentarily distracted him from the conversation. I watched as he scoffed at the screen before furiously typing a response. All interest in the football game on the television completely lost. I heard giggling from the other room, signifying my mother and Kellan up to something that I could only hope wouldn't involve me. My father sat at the kitchen island, partially in view from where I was sitting. He watched the two of them with a bemused smile on his face.

"For Christ's sake!" Montrell exclaimed, tossing the phone beside him on the couch.

"Restaurant troubles?" I asked. Montrell was the owner of one of the most popular restaurants in town. The Hungry Hippo. He started it when he was in college, by selling plates out of his apartment. From there, he progressed to a food truck and now an entire restaurant. It started as just a side gig to earn money while he was in school, but ended up unlocking a passion for food and cooking that has followed him ever since. His degree in business helped him get started, but it was the love and passion for creating meals that could bring people together that pushed him as far as he is now. His decision to go back to culinary school only strengthened the skills he'd already had. As much as I hated to admit it, since it would do nothing but soup his head up, the man was talented in the kitchen.

"Yeah, man. I told you I have to work on the new menu for the Christmas season. It's been difficult."

"That's right. You still in competition with that other restaurant?" It was a simple question, but the way his eyes darkened at the mention of Audrey Bennett's popular eatery made me almost regret asking.

"There is no *competition*," he spat defensively. "Her restaurant is purely gimmick and niche. The talent is not there! Her food is-"

"My bad bro. Whatever you say." I interrupted, throwing my hands up in mock defeat.

I could tell he wanted to say something else in protest, but I changed the subject before he made me an unwilling participant in the newest rant about Audrey's Kitchen. It wouldn't be the first time. I'd been to her restaurant a few times, and I didn't see what bothered him so much about the place. If I was being honest, she was a pretty good cook. Her breakfast crepes were absolutely out of this world. She's just as good, if not better, than Montrell. He would lose his mind if he ever found out that I'd eaten there, let alone if I ever said that out loud, so I kept it to myself.

"Did I tell you I'm working on this Christmas musical this year at my school?" He shot me an incredulous look.

"Since when do you get involved in Christmas plays? You hate Christmas."

"I do not *hate* Christmas! It's just not my favorite. Anyway, the principal asked me to help out this year because the English teacher is directing and she'll need some assistance."

I turned away from him, focusing my attention on the football game so he wouldn't see the look on my face, but he caught it anyway. He studied me for a moment, a smug expression forming.

"She? Is it that girl you mentioned to me before? Melody something?"

"Her name is Elodie, and yes. She's directing this year."

I tried to sound nonchalant, but the knowing smile on Montrell's face told me he saw right through it. I wanted to slap the irritating grin off, but I stared at the television instead.

Choosing not to resort to violence, even though thumping him in the forehead would be incredibly satisfying.

"That makes more sense. So, what will she have you doing? Parading around in a Santa Suit singing Christmas songs?"

I laughed and flipped him off. "I'm in charge of the music. I wanted to get a few things written."

"You're writing new songs for a Christmas play full of kids?" Montrell asked. The skepticism in his voice matched the expression on his face. "It's a middle school, Khi, not Broadway."

I rolled my eyes. "I'm aware of that. I'm not rewriting the words. Just changing the arrangements around. The same Christmas tunes every year can get boring."

I could feel him watching me, but I wouldn't give in. Kellan came bounding into the living room a moment later, briefly saving me from Montrell's scrutinizing gaze. Excitement poured off him in waves. I turned, just as my mother entered the room wearing a similarly excited grin.

"Your mom says we can decorate for Christmas tonight!" He practically shouted. "Can we please?!" I had never seen him so excited. Most of his enthusiasm could be attributed to the multiple slices of cheesecake he had just consumed. So much sugar in such a small frame was bound to have him crashing later on. I glanced over at Montrell, who had gone back to texting, no longer interested in the conversation happening around him.

"Really?" I asked. "She said tonight?" I raised an eyebrow at my mother, hoping she would catch the hint.

"Yes. I compromised and waited until after Halloween. I want my Christmas decorations out of the attic." She glared at me with a raised eyebrow. The look that told me she wasn't joking around. With a sigh, I reluctantly got up from the couch and turned to Montrell, who was still barely paying attention.

"Let's just go ahead and do it before she beats me with a candy cane," I grumbled. A triumphant smile softened her features. I could see why her smile made my dad putty in her hands. It brightened up the room every single time. I made fun of him many times over the years for being powerless to resist her demands, but here I was, pulling the string connected to the attic stairs so I could get the decorations. No stronger than he was.

By the time we brought down all the boxes and stacked them in various corners of the living room, an hour had passed. Kellan sat with my father watching football while he explained everything that was happening. Dad never missed a chance to teach someone about football, even if his pupil was an unwilling participant. Kellan, however, looked completely enthralled with every word that came out of his mouth. He asked questions and paid close attention, as if what my father was saying contained valuable information he would need later.

As I stacked the last box of decorations labeled "bathroom decor" next to its assigned door, my thoughts drifted to Elodie. Again. I couldn't help but wonder what she was up to. Was she with her family? Was she reading? I'd overheard her talking with a few of the other teachers about a book club she was in with her friends from college. I was curious to know what kinds of books they were reading.

"Bro, just text her." Montrell's voice snapped me back to the present.

"What?"

He smirked. "Your eyes keep glazing over every time you start thinking about her. Stop obsessing and just text her."

I pulled out my phone and scrolled to her contact information. The name and number sat there on the screen taunting me. I wasn't sure why I was so nervous. We had a good time working together at the homeless shelter. I'd had no problems speaking to women in the past, even ones I found attractive, but there was something about her that made me question myself. She intrigued me and scared me at the same time.

If I texted her and invited her out on a date, would she say yes? She seemed interested enough at the shelter, but I couldn't be too sure. When I'd commented on her having a lot of love to give and wanting to see it up close, she didn't run screaming into the distance like I had been scared she would as soon as the words left my mouth. I swallowed back the lump forming in my throat and sent a quick message before I could find a reason to talk myself out of it. The worst she could say was no, and then I would know exactly where we stood. After I picked my ego off the floor, I'd be able to keep the relationship strictly professional if it called for it.

To my surprise, she was receptive. She took it a step further than what I was expecting and offered to come to the house instead of going out to make sure that Kellan was comfortable. I debated letting him hang out here with my parents. I'm sure they would love the company, but just as quickly as the thought popped up, I pushed it away.

The last thing I wanted to do was dump Kellan off on someone else like he was some type of burden, even if my parents would be delighted to spend more time with him. Elodie coming over to the house wouldn't be a problem. Right? The idea made me nervous. As much as I wanted to spend time with her, Kellan had to be my top priority while he was with me. It seemed like Elodie understood that.

"Hey! Don't leave us to do all the work, Mekhi Davis!" My mother's voice sounded stern, but when I glanced up at her, she was smirking. After texting Elodie my address, I put my phone back in my pocket and stood, stretching.

"Can I take a raincheck?" I asked, picking up a bulb from the open box nearest the couch. It was silver and blue with glittery snowflakes; it used to be part of an identical group of ornaments, but between Montrell and I manhandling the decorations throughout the years, this was the only one left.

"Raincheck denied." She tossed a pillow at my head. I ducked, laughing at her attempt to catch me off guard. Kellan watched our interaction with a look on his face that I couldn't read. His eyes were sullen and withdrawn, a stark difference from the joy I had seen in his expression just moments earlier.

Before I could address it, Montrell popped up behind him and placed a Christmas hat he had grabbed out of one of the boxes on Kellan's head. It was red with green stripes and obnoxious elf ears sticking out of the sides.

"Gotta have the appropriate attire to decorate the tree, man." He said, clapping Kellan on the back.

"Can I put the star on the tree?"

A glance passed between my parents and me. It had always been my mother's job to place the star on the tree. It was something she took seriously, almost too seriously, every single year. No one was allowed to touch the star. It was a gift that had passed down through the generations in her family and something she fiercely protected. With a smile and a small nod, she turned to Kellan, who was staring up at the seven-foot-tall fake tree that stood in the corner of the living room, waiting to be decorated. He was completely oblivious to the silent conversation happening around him. My mother placed an arm around his shoulders and squeezed.

"You absolutely can."

"Did you have a good time?" I glanced over at the groggy preteen curled up in the passenger seat. He still wore the Christmas hat, one of the elf ears folded up under where he rested his head on the headrest. His eyelids drooped sleepily, but the smile on his lips warmed my heart.

"Your family is fun." He said quietly, snuggling deeper into the seat. The seatbelt rested against the side of his cheek.

I smiled. "I don't know what kind of spell you put on my mom, but I'm sure she likes you more than me now."

"I'm cooler than you." A sleepy grin made the dimples in his cheeks appear. I snorted at his comment and turned my attention back to the road. A comfortable silence fell over the car. I had hoped that today would go well, but it had gone much better than I had hoped. Kellan fit right in with the family like he was always meant to be there.

He headed straight to his room to go to sleep when we arrived back at the house, leaving me to sit on the couch and let my mind spin. So much had happened in the past few days. Not only did I get a foster child that I wasn't expecting, but I was also finally able to connect with Elodie after watching her around the school for the last few weeks. This musical was the perfect opportunity for us to connect in a way that wouldn't be too much pressure for either of us.

I had been thinking about leaving after the holiday season. The plan had never been to stay at Astoria Middle School long term.

When I took the job, I had nothing keeping me here permanently and no interest in putting down any roots so quickly. It was meant to be temporary. I was only here until the next gig came around. I'd had a few offers to go back on the road and at first, it was a no-brainer, but now there was so much more to consider.

7

Elodie

"You're going over to his house?" It was Friday afternoon, an hour before I was supposed to meet Mekhi, and I had my girls on Facetime while I got ready. I had been fine until Mekhi texted me to confirm, and then my nerves started getting the better of me. According to the journal, we would really start to like each other. I wasn't sure if I was ready for that. The passage kept playing in my head, amplifying my anxiety and making me want to call the entire thing off. Luckily, my girls were all free to talk in the midst of their Black Friday shopping plans.

"Yes, Audrey. I'm going to his house. We need to get a jumpstart on the songs before school starts back Monday." I leaned towards my mirror and then froze. "Wait, is that weird?"

"Just make sure you put his address in the group chat. And update us periodically throughout the day. Don't make me have to come find you, because I will, and you know I will," Brina said, typing as she talked. Most likely working even though she had promised us she would take some time off.

I rolled my eyes. "Okay, Ms. Prosecutor. I will, I promise."

She stuck her tongue out at my comment. I always picked on her for being so paranoid, but I appreciated the reminder. If Mekhi did suddenly become a murderer and killed me like we were on an episode of Dexter, at least my friends would have his address and would be able to alert the authorities before my body got cold.

"Is this a date?" At Audrey's question, everyone turned to stare at me through their screens. I froze for a second, unsure of how to even answer. Was it a date? Or was it just two colleagues who had been forced to work on a project together, meeting to work on said project? Purely innocent and unromantic.

"We... are just friends," I replied, fidgeting with my hair and avoiding looking at my phone screen. The deafening silence that followed made my cheeks flush.

"Let me rephrase," Audrey shifted on her bed where she had her phone propped up in front of her, "Do you want this to be a date?"

I chewed my bottom lip. If I was honest with myself, I did want this to be a date. Mekhi was incredibly attractive and seemed like a nice guy from what I knew so far, but I wasn't sure how he felt. If I let the journal tell it, the feelings were mutual, but I was not about to make a move based on a magical phenomenon. That's a good way to get embarrassed.

"I wouldn't mind-"

Excited squeals erupted from all four girls, interrupting the rest of my thoughts. I laughed, "He seems sweet so far, but who knows how long that will last."

I didn't want to seem bitter, but my last few relationships had really soured me on the idea of dating. I couldn't help but look at this situation with a bit of pessimism. Mekhi almost seemed too good to be true and if my past was any indication, he probably was.

"Let's see your outfit. Give us a spin." Monae twirled her hand, indicating she wanted me to show off what I was wearing. I stepped back from the phone. I picked out a red plaid skirt, black knee-high boots, and a black sweater and paired it with Christmas tree earrings. Monae gave a nod of approval. She was always the one I went to for fashion advice. When she wasn't in her work uniform, the girl could style a trash bag and make it cute.

"Okay. We approve. It's giving Christmas, but not too over the top."

My gaze drifted over to the journal on my desk. The last entry still looping through my mind. I'd gone to sleep and then popped awake to read it again, just to make sure I wasn't dreaming. I wasn't. The same words I'd read last night waited for me this morning. I still wasn't fully sold on the idea of it being magical, even if it had been the subject of some unexplainable events. It felt creepy, like someone was watching me and updating the journal without my knowledge.

"So, what's up with the journal?" Deja asked, clearly reading my thoughts. "Do you really believe it's magical?"

"I know it sounds ridiculous, but you guys didn't see what I saw," I protested.

I could tell from the looks on their faces they were still skeptical. I couldn't even blame them. The next time it happened, I'd have to record it for proof. That was the only way they would believe that something was possessing this journal. Audrey was the only one who didn't seem to want to have me committed.

"What's wrong with believing in a little Christmas magic?" she said with a small shrug. "We could all use some, could we not?"

If I could hug her through the screen, I would have. I smiled gratefully at her. The other three nodded reluctantly, choosing to agree for the moment and let it drop.

"Besides," she continued, "I could use a little magic myself."

I grabbed my keys and headed out to the car, thankful for the shift in the conversation. Audrey filled us in on the trouble she was having with work. The owner of a competing restaurant, The Hungry Hippo, was giving her a lot of unnecessary flak. The two of them had been butting heads ever since the diner opened on the same street as her. It was an audacious move, opening a restaurant so close to an already successful one, but it had proven to work out in the owner's favor.

"This guy sounds like a jerk," I said after listening to Audrey vent about the latest issue. The others agreed. I felt bad for my friend. She had a passion for her business and for cooking that was now having to play second fiddle to the competition brewing between restaurants. She was so busy having to figure out ways to one-up him that she hadn't been able to devote enough time to trying new recipes like she wanted. And the shift in focus was taking its toll on her. Audrey was always reserved, but she seemed more withdrawn than usual.

I made a note to check on her later when I had more time to devote to a one-on-one conversation. If nothing else, I could at least see how I could be of support. Two heads were always better than one, and if we had to brainstorm ideas together to take this guy down, I would be all in. Anything to ease her stress a little. I ended the conversation with my girls so I could focus on the directions to Mekhi's place.

He lived in a nice-looking neighborhood. The residents on his street had already begun decorating for Christmas. Half-hung lights dotted the yards as I inched down the street, counting house numbers. My stomach had made its way to my throat, making me second guess everything from my shoes to my choice of earrings. I pulled up in his driveway and sat frozen in place, unsure of whether I should get out or text him and say that I was feeling sick and needed to reschedule. I had just decided on the latter when the front door opened and he stepped out.

My heart caught in my throat at the sight of him. He wore dark blue jeans and a winter green sweater. It was a simple outfit, but enough to make the butterflies swirl around in my stomach. His eyes locked on mine and a slow smile spread across his features. It did nothing to help my nerves. With a deep breath, I grabbed my belongs and then I opened my door, and then tumbled straight to the ground in a clumsy heap.

My foot had somehow gotten caught in the door and sent me spiraling to the concrete in a mess of limbs and plaid. I could feel my entire body flushing, but before I could pick myself up, two strong arms hooked themselves under my pits and pulled me to my feet.

"You alright?" Mekhi asked, examining me. His brows furrowed in concern, and I couldn't help but feel a wave of gratitude for his reaction. I would have had no choice but to evaporate into the gravel had he laughed at my fall. I nodded, feeling too embarrassed to speak right away, and made a show of wiping the dirt off my clothes.

"Physically, sure. But my ego hasn't taken a hit like that in a while." It wasn't until I turned to face him that I realized he was still holding my arms. I glanced down at his hands quickly, wondering what they would feel like against my skin before shoving the thought away and forcing a smile. "Thanks for helping me up."

He nodded and cleared his throat, dropping his arms back at his sides and leaving me suddenly feeling cold without the heat of his touch. His gaze drifted over my shoulder, and I turned to see Kellan peering at us from inside the house. When he noticed us looking, his head immediately disappeared from the window. I laughed, letting that momentary distraction break the tension between us.

"How is he doing?" I asked.

"So far, so good. My mom made a show of spoiling him yesterday. I'm pretty sure he's already a part of the family in her head."

"That's so sweet, though. Kids really just want to feel included." I replied, looking around for my phone before spotting it in the grass a few feet away. I grabbed it, trying hard to seem like I wasn't still embarrassed about face planting in front of his house. If Mekhi was judging me for falling, he gave no signs. Instead, he motioned for me to head to the front door.

I stepped inside and looked around. I had half expected his home to be empty aside from a television and a singular seating option like most bachelor pads I had been in, but I was pleasantly surprised. There was an entire living room set, the color of a luxurious espresso. A large house plant sat in the corner with unique art pieces on the walls across from the television. It was minimalistic, but in a tasteful way. Monae would get a kick out of the color scheme. An espresso brown with a deep, serene shade of green.

"Is green your favorite color?" I asked. Mekhi chuckled softly from somewhere behind me. I hadn't realized he had been watching me as I took in his decor.

"Is it that obvious?" I motioned to his sweater and then pointed at the other shades of green in the room. He nodded, the smile making itself at home on his lips. "Yeah, I guess it is."

"Mine is wine red," I replied. "Not that you asked."

Before he could respond, Kellan peeked around the corner and waved shyly. "Hi, Ms. Banks."

"Hi Kellan." I was shocked by his timidity. In class, Kellan was loud and unafraid to commandeer the conversation. He always was the center of attention among his friends and other classmates. Here, he seemed like a completely different person.

"You have dirt on your butt."

I blinked, surprised, "Huh?"

He pointed, his cheeks flushing a deep red. "You have dirt on your butt." He repeated.

The embarrassment from earlier that I had managed to stifle, surged back up to the surface, making me want to run and hide. So far, this day was not going how I planned.

"The bathroom is to your right, if you want to... um... freshen up a bit?" Mekhi glared at Kellan quickly before pointing in the direction of the bathroom. "We'll be in the last room on the left when you're ready."

"Was I not supposed to say anything?" Kellan hissed as Mekhi lightly pushed him forward. I heard him mumbling in protest as they walked further down the hall. I'd definitely have to fill my girls in later on how I've only been at his house for five minutes and felt enough embarrassment to last for the next two months. I could already hear Brina snickering at my expense.

After cleaning myself off, I followed the sound of the piano to the back room. Mekhi sat at the piano playing a beautiful tune while Kellan stood next to him, staring in awe at the way his fingers glided over the keys. I stood in the doorway for a moment, watching the two of them interact.

"Can you teach me how to play that?" Kellan asked, wide eyed. Mekhi nodded and continued to play the beautiful melody. Principal Ardell had mentioned he was talented, but this was my first time witnessing it for myself. He played effortlessly, his fingers jumping from key to key. The longer I listened, the more I could recognize what he was playing. It was "Best Part" by Daniel Caesar and H.E.R. One of my favorite songs.

"I love this song," I said, stepping completely into the room. Both looked up at the sound of my voice.

"It's already a good song. I just put my own spin on it." Mekhi replied with a small shrug. He acted as if it was no big deal. Out of the corner of my eye, I saw Kellan glancing between the two of us. I smiled over at him, still feeling a twinge of embarrassment from earlier.

"Are you helping with this Christmas production, Mr. Washington?" I asked, turning towards him. He nodded excitedly.

"Yeah! If Mr. D is cool with it. Can we sing You're a Mean One, Mr. Grinch? I can wear the costume." Kellan crept across the room in his best Grinch impression. He looked more like an old man with an injured leg. I watched, fully prepared to hype him up, but Mekhi spoke up before I could.

"We'd need to work on your Grinch impression."

Kellan stopped hobbling around the room and glared at Mekhi, his brow furrowed. "What's wrong with it?"

"It sucks." Mekhi replied with a shrug, "You have to do it like this!" Kellan and I both watched in amusement as Mekhi folded his large, burly frame into an obnoxious hunched position and hobbled forward in a Grinch-like fashion. Kellan followed suit, leaving me the only one in the room not trying to copy the Grinch's silly behavior.

I couldn't help but laugh watching the two of them. Watching the two of them together, you would have thought Kellan had been here longer than a few days.

"Alright, I think we have gone over enough to take a break now," Mekhi said, tapping the pencil he had been scribbling notes with on his lips. Kellan threw his hands up in a dramatic show of relief and collapsed on the floor.

"FINALLY!" He screeched, "We've been doing this for like forever hours!"

"It's been two," I laughed, even though I was also grateful for the rest. Mekhi was intense when it came to music. We had spent the entire two hours figuring out the best Christmas songs to perform and the best order to perform them in. Watching him concentrate so hard on the sheet music of the songs we had chosen while he tweaked the notes a bit more to his liking was fascinating. His entire body tuned into each note, no matter how simple the song was.

Watching him play the piano felt almost sensual in a way I hadn't expected. I found myself staring as he played, transfixed by the way his fingers glided over the keys and wondering how those same fingers would feel against my skin. The thought had made me blink in surprise and then embarrassment when I realized Kellan had been watching me stare at Mekhi with a goofy smirk on his face.

"You hungry, kid?" Mekhi asked, interrupting my inappropriate thoughts. His question was directed at Kellan, but when I glanced up, I was surprised to find him watching me.

"Duh!"

"Go ahead to the kitchen and get the table set up. We can have a quick lunch."

"Okay!" Kellan looked over at me. "You coming?"

Before I could answer, Mekhi placed a hand on my arm. "We'll be there in a second." He replied, his dark eyes studying my face. Kellan shrugged and left the room, letting the door close softly behind him.

"Is everything okay?" I asked gently, after a moment of complete silence had passed. There were so many emotions dancing across his face and even though I had wanted to know what he was thinking behind each one, I kept my questions to myself. Mekhi's gaze drifted down to my lips, pausing there for a moment before meeting my eyes again.

"Yes," he paused, "I just wanted to say thank you for suggesting and being so cool about coming here to meet with me instead of somewhere else. I know it probably felt a little rushed coming to my house on the first link up."

"That's okay. It's a delicate situation, I understand." My voice came out in a whisper, afraid to break the moment by speaking in full volume. As I spoke, his gaze shifted back down to my lips as if he was memorizing their movements with each word. This sudden shift in vibe made me feel slightly dizzy. One minute we were practicing as if nothing was wrong and the next, we were standing toe to toe, staring at each other like the first meal after a fast.

"If things were different, I would have taken you out properly first before-"

"Like a date?" I blurted, interrupting. Mekhi paused for a moment, considering my question, before he let out a laugh.

"Yes, Elodie. A date. Unless I am imagining this vibe."

He raised an eyebrow. I bit my lip, trying and failing to keep from smiling. As he and I stood there, whispering to keep from being overheard by Kellan, I began feeling something similar to the green monster that had become a Christmas time favorite.

I could feel my heart growing three sizes.

Dear Diary

Something about being around Mekhi makes Elodie want more More time more laughing more moments of ease After tonight it s evident that she desires his presence rather than simply enjoying it There s a quiet comfort in the way he makes her feel seen and his presence seems to drown out everything else

They didn t say it but they both felt it the pull to spend more time together not just for the musical but for something deeper It s subtle but there The thought of seeing him again doesn t feel like something to be scheduled it feels like something to be anticipated

I stared at the words that had been waiting on the page for me when I arrived home. Annoyed that this thing kept working before I could pull my phone out and capture it and also scared at how accurate it was. I couldn't tell if it was genuinely happening or if the journal was making me biased, but every time I was near

Mekhi it was like I couldn't get close enough. I couldn't stay long enough. I always wanted more.

I pulled out my phone, hoping that I wasn't the only one feeling something brewing between us. A message from Mekhi was already waiting for me when I clicked my phone screen. It was a picture he had secretly taken while Kellan and I were making lunch. It was a sweet picture, my head thrown back in a laugh while Kellan sang Santa Claus is Coming to Town loudly and off-key.

The text under the photo read: **You are the best part of this holiday season. Thank you.**

I stared at the message, feeling overcome with emotion. He was the best part of my holiday season so far as well. A few months ago, I had been positive that I would spend the holidays writing, reading, and occasionally spending time with my family. This was a wonderful change of plans.

So, about this proper date you were supposed to take me on...

I patted Bark Twain on the head while I waited for Mekhi's response. He wagged his tail and stared at me with his big, round eyes. His pink tongue lolled to the side lazily. The Hallmark Channel played a random Christmas movie with Tia Mowry that I vaguely remembered seeing before, but never getting the chance to finish.

I'm listening...

I've always wanted to try ice skating. Let's go tomorrow night. I can bring my dog, Bark Twain.

Instead of texting me back, Mekhi called me. I picked up the phone, smiling from ear to ear. We had just seen each other, but I missed him already. Hearing the sound of his voice soothed something in me.

"Is your dog actually named Bark Twain?" I could tell he was smiling.

"Yes. I'm an author. It makes sense." My response was met with laughter. It was an infectious sound. I found myself smiling even harder.

"Ridiculous." He snorted. I heard Kellan whooping excitedly in the background. "But, if you can't already tell, we would love to go ice skating with you."

"Great," I replied, "It's a date."

8

Mekhi

"Mr. D, can we practice some more songs tonight? I think I'm really getting the hang of God Rest Ye Merry Gentlemen." Kellan tugged on his coat and smiled hopefully. He had been catching on quicker than I expected. When he wasn't playing with the PlayStation, he was scrolling through YouTube videos looking at piano tutorials. Whatever he couldn't figure out by watching the video, he would ask me to step in and help. We spent most of the day going over the songs we had picked for the musical and, to my surprise, he was able to play them well, even with the changes I'd made to the notes.

"Sure."

"Do you think Ms. Elodie can come over tonight?" He asked, shyly. "I like her."

I smiled down at him. "Me too, kid."

We stood in the middle of the town commons, waiting for Elodie to arrive. She'd texted me earlier to ask our shoe sizes so she could bring the ice skates and to tell me she was excited to see us. Kellan stuffed his hands in his pockets and shivered, the cold making his nose and cheeks flush a light pink. A couple whizzed by us, holding hands. Kellan studied them for a moment, then turned to me, a look of determination on his face.

"I'm going to skate that fast."

"Have you ever ice skated before?" I asked, trying not to laugh at his seriousness.

"No. But watch me! I'll be fast."

I felt a tingle in my spine, and I looked up to see Elodie walking towards us, a small fluffy black dog following closely behind her. Her curls were tied in a pineapple with tendrils framing her face. Her cheeks were already red from the cold, a black bag bounced against her back with each excited step. I watched her, stunned at the physical reaction my body had to being in her presence. I'd felt her near me before I laid eyes on her. That had never happened before.

"Hello, sirs." She grinned. "I'd like you to meet my son, Bark Twain." The little dog circled excitedly around Kellan's feet, tail wagging wildly.

"Puppy!" Kellan shrieked, just as excited.

"Looks like they like each other." She whispered, squeezing my hand. Warmth sizzled on my skin under her touch, momentarily distracting me. I smiled back at her and nodded at the ice skates she'd slung over one shoulder.

"Need help with those?" A group of kids skated past us, giggling loudly while Kellan focused his attention on Bark Twain. Who seemed more than happy to be the star of the show. Elodie untied the skates, handed me my pair, and gave the other pair to Kellan.

"Have you ever tried ice-skating?" She asked me. I slid my feet inside the skates and stood on wobbly legs. Any hopes of impressing her with my gracefulness long gone. She watched me struggle, a small smile pulling at the corner of her mouth. "I'll take that as a no."

When we were all wearing our skates and Bark Twain donned his fuzzy boots to protect his paws, we all stepped out onto the ice. True to his word, Kellan raced around the rink, catching on quicker to the concept than I expected. Couples and families with small children zipped around, their faces full of smiles and excitement. I'd never been one for cliche Christmas behavior, but being out here with Elodie, Kellan, and that dog with the silly name made me rethink. Seeing Kellan smiling from ear to ear as Elodie flailed around clumsily in her skates warmed my heart in a way I hadn't thought possible.

"Watch this, Mr. D!" Kellan shouted, attempting a twirl. He landed awkwardly and then shot his hands up in the air in a celebratory motion.

He grinned proudly. "Ta-daaaaa!"

"Nice job, kid." I laughed. My shins burned mercilessly with every lumbered step. Thin beads of sweat dotted my forehead, even though it was cold outside. It'd been so long since I wore a pair of skates that I'd completely forgotten what a leg workout it was. I looked around, spotting an empty bench a few meters away, and hobbled towards it. Elodie following closely behind.

"Looks like you had the same idea I did." She grinned breathlessly, plopping down on the bench to take off her skates. She reached around to pull our shoes out of the bag. I gratefully grabbed mine and flopped down next to her, the burning in my legs calming slightly.

"I'm getting too old for this kind of excitement." I huffed.

We watched as Kellan flew around the rink, making friends with a few of the kids out there with him. Bark Twain ran happily behind them, carefully dodging some of the clumsier skaters.

"How is he adjusting?" I heard Elodie ask. I turned to see her watching him as well.

"He's doing great so far. The Forever Families program he's in sets him up with great resources." I replied.

"What's Forever Families?"

"It's the new foster program the state is working on. He's part of the pilot program. They set him up with placements and make sure he gets support on his education and extracurriculars. Something to make sure he gets the most success."

"I didn't realize he was in that type of program. It sounds like it could help so many kids." Elodie looked out at the rink while she talked, smiling as Kellan zipped past us with an excited wave.

"It's a great program. They're struggling to find funding currently." I replied. "I'm glad he's able to participate while it's still running. Kellan is a dope kid. His music is improving even quicker than I thought it would."

"You sound like a proud dad."

"I am proud of him." I purposely ignored the dad comment. "He reminds me a lot of myself. Especially with the music. I clung to it when I was his age. It got me through some tough nights."

"Tough nights?" Elodie asked, leaning forward.

"Yeah. Didn't always have it the easiest growing up."

Before I could elaborate on what I meant, Kellan came skating over, carrying Bark Twain in his arms. His cheeks were flushed from exertion and from the cold, but his eyes were bright with joy.

"Guys! One of my classmates is here, and he told me his parents are taking him to the light show in the next town over. Can we go?! It's free!" His words tumbled out in a jumble of eagerness. His happiness was infectious. I found myself smiling just because. I turned Elodie, the question already in my eyes before I spoke.

"Sure." she shrugged, reaching out to give her dog a quick scratch behind the ears. "But only if you drive."

All four of us piled into my truck while Kellan chattered excitedly about a conversation he'd had with his friend while he was on the ice. I was only half listening, more focused on the scent of Elodie's perfume that lingered every time she moved past me. It was an intoxicating scent and singlehandedly ruining my ability to concentrate on anything else.

"The tour starts in an hour. I Googled the address; it'll only take us thirty minutes to get there. So that gives us plenty of time!" Kellan announced, pulling Bark Twain into his lap. The two had become fast friends.

"Someone is excited." Elodie smiled from the passenger seat and turned to look at the two of them.

"It's supposed to be really cool!"

I put the address in my GPS and used every ounce of willpower I could muster to keep my attention on the road. Elodie looked down at her phone for a second before clicking around on the Spotify that displayed on my car screen.

"Kellan, what's your favorite Christmas song?" she called over her shoulder.

"Grinch!" He replied without pausing for a moment to consider the question. She clicked through the songs until she found that one and pressed play. Thurl Ravenscroft's burly voice filled the speakers in my truck. Kellan yipped and began singing along as loudly as he could.

The two of them took turns singing Christmas songs at the top of their lungs while Bark Twain howled along, and I pretended to be annoyed by the noise. Truthfully, I was enjoying myself, even if I would never admit it out loud.

"Come on Mekhi, sing along! I know you know this one." Elodie prompted, turning the music up even louder.

"Absolutely not. Ya'll got it." I shook my head, stifling a laugh.

When we finally pulled up to the beginning spot for the Christmas light tour, their impromptu concert had calmed down. It left the car feeling deadly silent, but it was a silence I didn't mind. A bright tunnel of Christmas lights lay ahead of us, waiting for the signal to begin. In the few minutes since we'd pulled up, multiple cars had filled in behind us.

"Wow. This is already beautiful." Elodie whispered.

"It is," I replied quietly, but my gaze was fixed on her. Something in my tone caught her attention, and she turned to look at me, meeting my eyes with a curious expression. When our eyes locked, it felt like the world tunneled around us. Everything else around us disappeared. Her eyelids lowered as her gaze began to heat. I bit my lip, wanting nothing more than to lean forward and kiss her.

"Guys?" Kellan's confused voice called out. "It's starting!"

I cleared my throat awkwardly as Elodie shifted in her seat, pressing her legs together tightly. I clocked the movement, throwing her a knowing smile before pulling forward and letting the light show begin.

From the rearview mirror, I could see Kellan and Bark Twain with their noses pressed against the window, gawking at the lights. Everything around us was covered in Christmas lights of all shapes and colors, making it so bright outside that it felt like mid-afternoon. Elodie leaned her head against the seat and looked out, taking in the sight around her. I looked through the windshield, impressed with the set up.

Elodie's fingers brushed quickly against my hand, resting on the gearshift. I gently grabbed her hand and brought it up to my lips, letting them linger against the soft skin. Through the reflection of her window, I could see her eyes close as she sucked in her bottom lip. I pressed forward, wanting Kellan to have enough time to enjoy the lights, but tempted to rush so I could get Elodie somewhere private. I'd let her know exactly how hard I was fighting to behave myself.

This girl was going to drive me crazy.

"Did you have fun?" We were back at my place, letting Kellan settle in for the night. Elodie held her dog in her arms, finally getting him back after being abandoned for Kellan all night.

He nodded and yawned. "Yeah! Can we do it again?"

"Sure." I replied. "Maybe next week we can-"

"No, I mean next year." He interrupted. I froze, unsure of what to say.

Elodie glanced at me, sensing my panic. "It would be fun to start a tradition, wouldn't it? Makes the holidays more fun to look forward to. My family and I have a ton of traditions."

Kellan nodded as he slid further into his covers, letting sleep take over. Elodie and I turned out the light and backed out of his room, but as soon as I reached for the door, Kellan's eyes opened.

"Mr. D?" He called uncertainly.

"Yeah?"

"I really love it here."

"I love having you here." I could feel myself getting choked up. "Get some rest." I closed the door gently behind me, wondering how he had managed to sneak his way into my heart so quickly.

9

Elodie

Deary Diary

As Elodie rode through the light tour with Mekhi and Kellan the glow of Christmas lights draped over the trees casting a soft magical light around them The crisp air nipped at the windows but they barely noticed The warmth between them made the cold outside feel distant Kellan pointing out his favorite displays with an excitement that brought a smile to both their faces

Mekhi glanced at Elodie and when she met his eyes her heart caught in her chest In that brief moment it became clear how much she had come to care for both him and Kellan in such a short time It wasn t just the time spent together or the shared laughter it was *the feeling of belonging that was beginning to take root*

Under the canopy of twinkling lights surrounded by the sound of Kellan's oohs and aahs mixed with the dog's happy whimpers Elodie felt a warmth spread through her This wasn't just a fleeting moment it was something more Something she desperately wanted to hold on to

"Welcome back, Ms. Banks. How was your holiday?" Principal Ardell leaned against the doorway of my classroom while I set the room up for the lesson. Coming off of a holiday would have my students' attention span on zero, so I didn't plan anything heavy. Just a quick review before we needed to start preparing for exams.

"Thanks. It was great to have a few days off."

"Have you been able to connect with Mr. Davis about the musical?" She asked. I smiled to myself. Mekhi and I were definitely able to connect. My mind drifted back to the look he gave me in the car while we waited for the light tour to start. The heat in his gaze had made my insides clench in a way that felt incredibly inappropriate for someone I had recently met.

"Um... Yes. We were able to connect. Our first practice is after school today." I squeaked, feeling myself blush. "That was actually what I wanted to talk to you about."

She lifted a perfectly manicured eyebrow. "Oh?"

"Yeah. Have we picked the charity to donate to this year?"

"Not yet."

"What about Forever Families?" I watched as she contemplated my suggestion. I'd known since the moment Mekhi mentioned it that I would suggest it to Principal Ardell.

"I'm not sure I've heard of it."

"It's a foster program that helps children find placements. They provide temporary placements for those who need them and offer resources to make sure each child is set up for the best chance of success. One of my students is currently in the program." I wasn't sure how much she knew about Kellan's situation, but she seemed to pick up on what I was saying.

"I'll look into it. The kids are in charge of selling tickets, so I want you and Mekhi to focus on making this musical the best it can be. I will take care of the rest." She turned on her pencil heels and clicked down the hallway, leaving me with a few moments of peace before the students started arriving.

"Hey." I turned to see Mekhi standing in my doorway, a small smile on his lips.

I smiled back. "Hey yourself."

He stepped further into the room, revealing a small giftbag he had been hiding behind his back. "I got you something."

Inside the bag was a candle with "she's writing a bestseller" on the front in black letters and a pair of earrings in the shape of Candy Canes. Before I could catch myself, I stood up and threw my arms around his neck. He slipped his arms around my waist and pulled me closer to his body.

"Thank you," I breathed. "This was so thoughtful."

The bell rang, cutting our conversation short and letting us know first period was about to start. Disappointment flooded through me. I wanted more time with him.

"I'll see you after school." He squeezed my hand and then slipped out of the classroom just as my students started pouring in. The smoky smell of his cologne lingered even after he was gone.

"Alright guys, you know the Christmas play is going to be in a few weeks. Please sign your name on the sheet if you're interested in participating." Anxiety churned in my stomach as I passed around the sign-up sheet once everyone had been seated. "And please, for the love of God, write so I can actually read your name!"

I wasn't surprised by who signed up and who didn't. Zi'Ell and Sincerity were the first two in my class to sign up, barely taking time to read the line at the top about the frequency of the practices. Mitsi hesitated, but eventually signed up after giggling and whispering with her friends. I knew she had a little crush on

Zi'Ell and most likely wanted to use this play as an excuse to be around him more often.

He had a wonderful singing voice, and he used it to flirt with the other students in my class instead of paying attention. With some nurturing and practice, he had enough raw talent to make it far.

"How was your Thanksgiving, Ms. B?" He asked as he passed the sign-up sheet behind him for the next student to grab. I leaned against the front of the desk and folding my arms. The round lights on the Christmas sweater I wore snagged against the Christmas Tree charms on my bracelet.

"It went well, but I'm ready for Christmas now." I grinned and jingled my wrists to make my point. My students knew how much I loved Christmas. I'd had a countdown on the wall in my classroom since August. They'd take turns moving the dial on it to point out how close we were getting to the beloved holiday. It had become a fun tradition in my classroom.

I knew that some of my students came from lower income homes and didn't always get to participate in traditions like other families did. So, I liked to come up with fun ways to bring in the holiday spirit while they were here. I decided a long time ago to make it a point to invest in these little things. Even if they never admitted how much it meant to them, I could see it on their faces. That's what matters the most at the end of the day.

Zi'Ell rolled his eyes, the deep dimples in his cheeks visible from a mile away. "Yes, we know." The rest of the class giggled at him. I shook my head. I felt no shame about my love for the holiday season.

"How many Christmas sweaters do you have, Ms. Banks?" a small voice asked from the back of the classroom. London, one of my shy students, was looking at me expectantly. She rarely spoke up; I could probably count on one hand how many times I had heard her voice since the beginning of the school year. She usually preferred to hide behind her curtain of red hair.

I smiled at her. "I could probably wear one every day for the next few weeks."

"My stepdad says that Christmas sweaters are for people who can't get laid. Is that true?"

Laughter rippled through the classroom. London's cheeks reddened with embarrassment.

"Chill!" I admonished, "No, London sweetie, that's not necessarily true."

"Ohh! That means you're gettin' some, doesn't it, Ms. B?!" Zi'Ell shouted. I narrowed my eyes at him without answering. A few of his friends laughed, but the look on my face sucked the humor out of the room.

"Don't push your luck, Zi."

"Yes ma'am. Sorry."

The last student to have the sign-up sheet brought it up to my desk. I looked it over, excited to see that a few students I hadn't expected to participate had signed their names. We'd have a decent turnout if everyone continued to participate until the concert.

The rest of the day flew by, with me glancing up at the clock every two minutes, counting down the seconds until I could see Mekhi again. I felt giddy at the idea of being in the same space as him. It'd been a long time since I'd felt so excited to see someone. I couldn't help but wonder if it was all genuine or due in part to the journal telling me that he would be someone important. Was I letting fate take over or taking it into my own hands? I couldn't tell.

With the last few students filing out of the classroom, I pulled out my phone to look through my personal emails. An email from my editor sent with high importance flashed like a warning light on my screen. She was probably pulling her hair out by now at my lack of response, but these last few days have monopolized my focus. How was I supposed to write when a magical phenomenon was telling me that the music teacher I'd seen in the hallway was supposed to be my love match?

I typed a quick response to the editor, promising to get her a draft of my novel in the next few days, and replied to a text in the group chat. Monae was filling us in on a wild call she'd just had to take during her shift. The danger she ran head first into as a firefighter always amazed me.

I stood and stretched, rolling my shoulders back to relieve the tension that had built since earlier. After practice, I owed myself a hot bath and time to relax. My bracelets jingled as I reached down to my toes.

"Wow." I looked up to see Mekhi standing in front of me, looking me over like he wanted to have me for dinner. Both of us had made our feelings apparent, but neither of us had made a move yet. It was driving me crazy. All smoldering looks and lingering stares, but no action.

"How was your day?" I asked, fiddling with my bracelet. I suddenly felt nervous.

"It just got better." He grinned. "Where do you get these sweaters?" He flicked one of the lights attached to my stomach area and shook his head. I rolled my eyes but found myself unable to hide my smile.

"Why? You want one?"

"I'd rather not blind myself." He laughed. "I came to see if I could walk you to practice."

"Do you think I'll get lost between here and the auditorium?"

He shrugged. "It's hard to see where you're going with lights flashing in your face."

The banter between us was so comfortable, like we had known each other for years. I grabbed my things and locked my classroom door, debating whether or not I should tell him exactly what I was feeling.

10

Mekhi

"Who wants to touch my *jingle balls*?!" One kid, I think his name was Zi'Ell, screeched across the auditorium. A chorus of giggles erupted through the groups of students who had made a little circle in one of the farther corners of the room. Zi'Ell was a clown, but his fellow students seemed to really enjoy his antics. Especially his female classmates. I'd heard them giggling about how cute they thought he was more than once. I sighed, exhausted, and turned back to the piano. My focus was waning after a long day back at school. The first day back after a holiday break was always one of the rowdiest, even if it was just a few days. Clearly, it didn't take long for the routines that had been established in the earlier parts of the school year to be completely forgotten.

This was our first official practice after coming back from Thanksgiving break and I could already tell that Elodie and I were going to have our hands full with this bunch. From the moment practice had started, we spent more time trying to round up their attention than we did discussing the actual Christmas program. The two of us had talked about how it would be difficult the first couple of days, but neither one of us had expected just how difficult it would actually get.

I glanced up at her, willing myself not to stare too hard. She stood next to Alex, the math teacher, fixating on a part of the set. Her silly Christmas sweater, complete with a battery pack of Christmas lights, did nothing to dampen her beauty. Ever since I had made a bold move and acknowledged the obvious attraction between us, I hadn't been able to get her out of my mind. Whenever we weren't practicing, we were texting or finding silly excuses to see each other. We had seen each other every day since that first practice at my apartment. Each time her name popped up on my phone or I saw her smiling through the peephole on my front door, my heart jumped in my throat, like it was the first time I had seen her.

Even after she left that first night and Kellan proceeded to whoop my tail on my outdated version of 2k on the PlayStation, I couldn't get her scent of vanilla out of my nose nor her smile out of my head. I was grateful this Christmas production gave me even more of an excuse to spend time with her, even if we did have Kellan cock blocking the entire time. Just being in her space was enough for me. For now.

"Mr. Davis, did I tell you that my mom thinks you're hot?" Zi'Ell asked, breaking my thought process completely. Kellan and the other boys snickered behind him. I wanted desperately to join in on the laugh at his comment. I was fully aware of his mother's interest in me. She hadn't even bothered to hide her attraction, making sure to tip herself forward just enough to give me a full view down her shirt, but unfortunately for her, I had my sights set on one woman in particular. One woman who was completely covered head to toe in Christmas attire and unashamed of how silly it looked. I admired her commitment to the holiday. Even if that particular sweater looked super uncomfortable. I turned, fixing Zi'Ell with my sternest teacher glare, not wanting to encourage his silly behavior any more than his friends were.

"No, and I'm going to pretend I didn't just hear you say that."

Zi'Ell shrugged and turned back to his group of friends. Aside from Kellan, two other boys around their age huddled with them, whispering about one of the girls in the group of rows over. I'd miss this group when it came time for me to go back on the road,

Kellan especially. It had only been a few days of having him stay with me, but he fit in easily with my routine and having someone to keep me company was better than I had anticipated. His presence made my small house feel more like a home.

"Mr. Davis?" Elodie's voice snapped me out of my thoughts and sped up my heart. I pivoted in her direction, hoping she couldn't hear it thumping out of my chest. Math teacher Alex glared at me from where he now stood by himself, next to the stage decorations. His sudden animosity was interesting, but not enough to keep my attention from the perfection in human form in front of me.

"Yes, Ms. Banks?" I asked, my voice came out huskier than I intended. I coughed quickly, hoping none of the kids picked up on my tone. Elodie's cheeks flushed, telling me she heard exactly what I was trying hard to hide.

"Um... are you ready to rehearse the next song?" she asked, avoiding my gaze. I wanted to scoop her up in my arms and kiss her. These kids be damned, but I don't think that would bode well with the principal. Workplace relationships pissed her off more than most. She would probably be irritated to hear there were growing feelings between Ms. Banks and me. Even though I didn't care what any of them thought, from the way Elodie spoke of our coworkers, I could tell their opinions were important to her.

"Sure."

The kids lined up on stage one by one, ready to belt out the lyrics to The First Noel. Meanwhile, Alex skulked around in the background, setting up the decorations on stage and shooting a seething glare over his shoulder at me every few minutes. It seemed like he had a problem with me, but I wasn't sure what it could be. Nor did I care. If he wasn't going to voice his issue, then I wasn't going to bother with giving it any attention. He could stew in silence.

Elodie positioned herself in front and to the left of the piano, facing the kids. Her hair swished around her shoulders as she moved. A light whiff of gingerbread tickled my nose whenever she got close enough. The woman lived and breathed Christmas with an enthusiasm that would rival my mother, who, until now, had been the biggest elf I'd ever met. I found myself wanting to introduce her to my parents, just to see if they would get along. The thought made me trip over the piano keys. The note rang out in the auditorium like nails on the chalkboard. Elodie turned to me, confusion wrinkling her gentle features.

"You okay?" she asked quietly. How do I tell her that I was daydreaming about introducing her to my parents without sounding like I'd lost my mind? The group of kids snickered as I did my best to collect myself. Losing my grip on my thoughts like this was new. Especially in front of people.

"Yes, I'm fine," I replied with a tight smile. She studied me for a moment before nodding and turning back to the task at hand.

"Alright, from the top."

Three hours, four songs, and a group of grumpy seventh graders later, we were finally ready to wrap things up for the evening. Parents had begun filing in towards the end of the last song, waiting to pick up their children and head home. Alex stood off to the side, chatting happily with Elodie, who didn't look as interested in the conversation as he did.

"Mr. D!" Kellan came galloping over, one of his classmates in tow. I smiled at who I assumed was the kid's mother, walking up less enthusiastically than the two boys. "Can I hang out with Parker for a few hours? His mom said she would bring me home."

I was surprised that Kellan had shared with his friend that he was staying with me. I hadn't been sure how to navigate the situation once Thanksgiving was over and school was back in session; I didn't want to put Kellan's business out there just in case he was embarrassed about his current living situation, but from the looks of it, my caution was unnecessary.

"Sure. Only if it's okay with Ms..." I glanced up at the woman, leaving space for her to give me her name. She smiled at me, her almond skin flushing slightly under my gaze. She was a beautiful woman. I couldn't deny that. Her shapely curves were tucked into a sweater dress that hugged her in all the right places.

"Miss Sage." She offered, emphasizing the "miss" in her name. I nodded and turned back to the boys.

"Only if it's okay with Ms. Sage."

"It's perfectly okay with me. Kellan is a sweet kid." I swelled with pride at her response, even though Kellan wasn't biologically mine. These last few days with him had given me a glimpse of the intelligent, kind-hearted child that was hidden under his class clown behavior.

After making Kellan promise to text me if he needed to come home sooner than planned, I turned back to the piano to grab the notes I had made on the sheet music, only to be greeted by Alex standing closer to me than I appreciated.

"You good?" I asked, continuing to gather my things.

He crossed his pale arms over his thin chest and stared at me. "I heard you were leaving after this Christmas season is over."

"Who told you that?" I shifted my body to face him completely, choosing to leave my posture relaxed. He was no threat, even though he was trying his hardest to seem intimidating. He shuffled his feet uncomfortably and glanced away.

"We all know about your career as a fancy musician." Disdain dripped from his tone. I remained silent. "I just want you to be careful with Elodie. I see you drooling over her. She deserves to be happy and to be with someone who won't just leave her behind in a few months."

"Let me guess, that person, is you?" It was my turn to fold my arms. Alex visibly deflated, realizing his thinly veiled threat hadn't moved me in the slightest.

"No, I-"

"Listen, Andrew. I have no intention of hurting Ms. Banks, but I can appreciate your concern. It's unneeded though. If you'll excuse me." Before he could respond, I grabbed my things and approached Elodie, who had just waved at the last kid and their family. She turned to the sound of my footsteps, a bright smile on her gorgeous face.

"Where's Kellan?" she asked, glancing around.

"He's going to hang out with some friends for a bit. Are you hungry?"

"Starving, actually. Want to get something to eat with me?"

I blinked, surprised she beat me to the punch, before nodding and offering her my hand. "Absolutely."

She chewed her lip for a moment before gingerly placing her palm against mine. Her skin was soft and warm. I sucked in a deep breath, struggling to calm my flooding emotions. We had only recently started interacting, but there was so much I wanted to do with... and to her.

"I know the perfect spot."

Turns out, the "perfect spot" was Audrey's Kitchen. The same restaurant with the very same chef who had been the cause of my brother's stress and misery for months. He would lose his mind if knew I had even stepped foot in this restaurant, let alone dined here.

"They have the perfect Shrimp Etouffee here." Elodie practically gushed. She tightened her grip on my hand and yanked me past the greeter and over to a table in the corner.

"Wait, don't we have to be seated by someone?" I asked, throwing an apologetic glance over my shoulder at the hostess. Elodie scoffed and pointed towards the mauve shell chair. The color combination of this restaurant was unlike anything I had ever seen in person. The entire place looked like it was straight from an advertisement.

Geometric patterns on the wallpaper gave the entire place a modern but quirky feel. Black and white photos of African American artists occupied the walls. It was an impressive design, a modern take on an old-school diner. I could see why this place got under Montrell's skin so badly. It was unique. The owner clearly had an eye for style. If the food was anywhere near as good as the decor, he'd have stiff competition on his hands.

"Isn't this place great?" Elodie's smile was wide and full of delight. I studied her expression, taking note of the way her eyes practically disappeared into her cheeks when she smiled. A deep dimple on her left cheek made visible by her grin.

"It's dope so far. You eat here often?"

"It's my best friend Audrey's place." She admitted. "She's got great food, but her confidence has been a bit shaken by the new place that opened up recently."

I knew it well. She was talking about Montrell's restaurant. I had listened to a mind-numbing amount of one-sided conversation from him about how she was working to steal his business. I glanced down at the menu, unsure of how to respond.

"How long have you two been friends?" I busied myself with reading the options. Seafood gumbo, smothered chicken, all the options sounded incredible.

"Since college. Me, her, and my other friends Brina, Monae and Deja have a book club we call 'Novel-Tea.' It's a way for us to force ourselves to hang out since we all have wildly different lives."

"Ellieee!!!" a voice squealed. A young girl with box braids down to the middle of her back and a mouth full of braces came bounding over to our table. Elodie gave her a tight hug. "Audrey will be happy to see you. Maybe you can tell her to stop obsessing over this Christmas Calzone idea."

"What's a Christmas Calzone?" I asked.

"It's a S'mores Calzone that she cuts into the shape of a Christmas tree. It's really cute. She got the idea from our grandma," the girl said, flashing her braces in a cheesy smile.

I focused on the menu while the two of them caught up. From the snippets of conversation I was trying not to eavesdrop on; I figured out that this bubbly young girl was Anika, Audrey's nineteen-year-old cousin. I finally settled on what I wanted to order; smothered chicken. Elodie and Anika had wrapped up their quick chat, and Anika took our orders and then skittered off into the kitchen, leaving me alone with Elodie. I suddenly felt nervous with her curious eyes on me.

"What's on your mind?" I asked, trying and failing to hide my smile.

"What made you become a foster parent?" she asked. I had been expecting this question at some point.

"My brother and I were in foster care for a while, before our parents adopted us. We got lucky. A lot of kids don't have the same positive outcome in the system. So, I try to give back however I can. Even if that means being a temporary place for them to land while permanent placement is sought after."

"Wow," she breathed. "I had no idea you'd been through that. Kellan is lucky to be able to stay with you."

"My mom loves him already." I shook my head with a smile. "By the time we left on Thanksgiving, she had already started factoring him into her Christmas list."

"She sounds great. I'd like to meet her one day." Our eyes locked in a gaze that sent waves of heat down my spine. Images of her meeting my family and spending the holidays baking with my mom or fussing with my brother over food choices and decorating the tree with my dad danced through my head. How could I be so crazy about someone I've only recently met?

"I'd like that too."

11

Elodie

"So the journal just mysteriously has an entry of your interactions with Mekhi every time you look at it?" Brina's skepticism made me second guess my decision to call her in a panic after getting home from dinner with Mekhi. I had entered my bedroom to find the journal open again and the pen flying. When it finally stopped and I worked up the courage to get closer to it, a short blurb about the dinner I had just left was written in swirly script.

During my freakout, I grabbed my phone and called the last person who texted me. That just happened to be Brina. She listened to my frantic rambling, but as soon as I finished talking, the silence was deafening. Her painfully logical lawyer brain was considering my words.

"No, not every time I look at it. It happens after every time I see Mekhi. I know I sound silly, Brin, but I'm so serious right now."

"Girl, I don't know what to tell you. Ask your grandma. She's the one that gave it to you, right?" She had a point. She was the one that held on to this journal for years, waiting for the right time to gift me with its magic. Clearly, she had some idea of what this thing was capable of. I promised to call Brina back and hurriedly dialed my grandmother's number. She picked up on the third ring.

"Hi, sweet baby." She greeted me. Her gentle voice soothed my anxious nerves. "I was wondering when you would get freaked out enough to call."

I paused, surprised. "You knew I'd call?"

"Of course, child. I gave you a journal that is shrouded in magic and I know how your mind works. I'm honestly surprised you waited this long."

"I don't understand what's happening, Grandmada! This journal is possessed and as a woman of God, I can't have it in my house!"

Her chuckle ringing in my ears made me smile, even though I was being serious. It was creeping me out. It felt like someone was watching me live my life and I didn't like the way it felt. How did celebrities handle being constantly watched? It's no wonder so many of them ended up crashing out.

"Elodie, sweetheart, it's not a demon and your faith is not in jeopardy. At least not from the journal. If anything, it would be your absence in church on Sundays."

A soft ping made me pull the phone back and look at it. A text message from the man of the hour had popped up on my screen. Saved by the text. I put my grandmother on speakerphone and pulled up our thread. It was a picture of a very sad-looking tree with Kellan standing next to it, poking out his bottom lip in an exaggerated show of sadness. Hobby Lobby bags sat scattered at his feet.

Purchased a Christmas tree. Apparently, I chose the worst one. You interested in helping us fix it?

My face relaxed into a cheesy grin. I had been bugging Mekhi about getting Christmas decorations ever since I went over to his house for the first time. He'd pretended to not be interested in my points about making his place feel homier for Kellan, but he had obviously been listening. I could see even more bags in the corner of the photo. He had gone all out. The effort made me want to throw my arms around his neck and kiss him.

Absolutely. Be there soon. Send me you guys' Chinese food order.

"Elodie! I know you hear me talking to you!" My grandmother's sharp tone snatched me back to reality. Just that quickly, I had gotten so wrapped up in texting Mekhi that I'd completely forgotten I was on the phone.

"My bad, Grandmada. What were you saying?" I pulled open my closet door, looking for the tightest pair of jeans I owned. I spotted them, black and about a size too small, sitting in the corner of my closet. I reached for them, then shook my head, opting for a pair of fuzzy Christmas pajama pants instead.

"I said that the journal serves as a guide. So often, we skip the small moments in life. Those moments are more important than we give them credit for. Don't fight it, baby. Let love find you." Her words made me pause for a moment to soak in what she was saying. After thanking her and promising to stop freaking out about the journal, I hurried out to my car so I could get to Mekhi and Kellan as soon as possible. I was craving their presence, Mekhi especially. We hadn't kissed yet, but we had both openly expressed our mutual interest. It was hard not to be interested in him. Every time we spoke, I was able to peel back another layer and get a glimpse of who he was.

At work, the whispers about Mekhi and his attractiveness continued, but now with the bonus of hearing my name mentioned along with his. Our coworkers took notice of the fact that we were seen together during planning periods or during our breaks. I could tell a few of the women teachers were jealous, but I didn't care. The more time we spent together, the more I craved it. The more I needed to feel his eyes on me, studying my every move as if his life was dependent on it. I needed his lips, which seemed fixed in a permanent smile whenever he was near me. I needed to see the way his thick arms strained against the sleeves of his shirts whenever he folded his arms. I could stare at him all day. I could breathe his air all day and it made me feel so special to know he felt the same way.

When I'd finally made it to his house, three bags of Chinese food in tow, I had to slow down my footsteps. I was practically running to the door with excitement. I took a deep breath and then took slow and deliberate footsteps until I reached his door. It swung open before I could knock. Mekhi stood in front of me, looking good enough to eat in a black undershirt and grey sweatpants.

"Hey!" He smiled, reaching for the bags in my hand. "Thank you for this. I owe you one."

"Sorry it took so long," I replied, stepping in the house and taking off my shoes.

"It's no problem. I barely noticed that-"

"Not true! He's been standing by the door looking out the window ever since you agreed to come!" Kellan shouted from the living room. I couldn't help but laugh at the mortified expression on Mekhi's face at Kellan's comment. He shook his head as he unwrapped the containers of food.

"He's exaggerating."

"No, I'm not!"

Mekhi glared at Kellan, who barely seemed to notice, as he came running into the kitchen to grab his food. My smile widened. Knowing he was so excited to see me made me feel good. Even if he was embarrassed to be called out so callously. I watched as the two of them argued like family while Mekhi fixed plates for the three of us. The Hobby Lobby shopping bags lay forgotten in small piles all over the living room floor.

"It looks like you went a little overboard with the decorations," I said, accepting the plate from Mekhi, "Unless your plan was to decorate your entire house."

"Would that be too much?" He paused to look at the bags, uncertainty in his expression.

"Not to me, but I'm probably the wrong person to ask. You know I love Christmas."

"I'd say that'd make you uniquely qualified to help." His smile was contagious. Just looking at the pure, unbridled joy on his face made me want to grab his cheeks in my hands and plant a kiss on his lips. I wondered what he would do if I did. I'd lost count of the times I'd caught him staring directly at my mouth like he was starving and couldn't wait to taste. The more we spent time together, the more I wished he would make that first move.

After making sure Kellan and I were situated, Mekhi fixed his plate and sat down next to me on the couch. I couldn't ignore how easily the three of us fit together like a puzzle that had finally found all of its pieces. My heart broke to know it would probably change after the holiday season was over and Kellan was put in permanent placement. Maybe whoever he ends up with will let us visit him.

We ate in comfortable silence while watching a cheesy Hallmark movie. I could tell that both Kellan and Mekhi were bored out of their minds with the predictable plot of the movie, but neither one protested. The credits rolled on the screen and I took that as my cue to get up and start looking through the decorations. Ornaments of all types of durability, shapes, sizes, and colors were stuffed into the bags. Garland, string lights, figurines, and snowflakes spilled out. Excess glitter sprinkled the carpet and the dining room chairs where the bags had been resting. It looked like Mekhi had spent a fortune on all this stuff, including the tree that had looked much smaller in the picture.

"You really went all out," I said, gingerly emptying the bags. Mekhi ran a hand over the back of his neck and shrugged sheepishly.

"Like you said, the decorations make the house a home. I wanted to make sure it felt like as much of a home as possible. Especially since-" He stopped short and shot a glance at Kellan, who was busying himself with finding a spot for the three reindeer figurines. We both watched silently as he placed them on the mantle above the fireplace and stepped back to admire his work.

"I just want him to have a good Christmas." His tone was soft, but his words were heavy. They carried the weight of his past life when he was in the system. He'd mentioned it when we went out for dinner the other day and I hadn't wanted to pry. It warmed my heart to know just how much he cared when he didn't have to. Being a teacher had a high propensity for burnout, as did social work, from what I had been told by friends who worked with the system. The fact that he had been so willing to open his home to a child in need when so many others had turned him away proved he was something special.

When his gaze met mine, my heart leapt in my throat. I hadn't expected to see so much longing and heat in a single look. I couldn't take it anymore. I grabbed Mekhi by the hand and dragged him down the hallway to the piano room. He seemed surprised, but didn't protest as I shut the door behind me and turned to him.

"This is driving me crazy." I breathed finally.

His brows knit together in confusion. "What is?"

Without responding, I stepped forward, placed my hand on the back of his neck and pulled myself up on my tiptoes so that our lips were barely an inch apart. His arms instinctively slipped around my waist and pulled me in even closer.

When our lips finally touched, I let out a small sigh of relief. He stepped forward until my back was against the door and deepened the kiss. I had fantasized about how his lips would taste and his hands would feel against my skin, and everything I had imagined paled in comparison to the real thing. His warm fingers pressed against the skin of my back gently, causing my entire body to tingle under his touch. I wanted more. Needed more.

"Elodie..." he groaned against my lips. I opened my mouth wider to invite his tongue inside. "Keep this up and I'll bend you over this piano right now."

I pressed myself even closer, feeling his growing erection through his sweatpants. I grabbed it gently and rubbed it through the fabric. It grew harder under my touch. He let out a low growl, tightening his grip on my waist with one hand and using the other to slide down my pajama bottoms. My core throbbed, dripping wet with desire. I opened my stance to allow him to enter and bit my lip as his skilled fingers pushed my panties aside and entered my most sensitive area. Fingers so skilled at making beautiful music rubbed against my clit in a way that made me dizzy and unable to catch my breath.

"God, you're soaked." He whispered, "All this for me, baby?" He'd been so gentle with me up until this moment. Now, in this room with him and his piano, all of the desire and lust behind his looks could finally be unleashed. Pure desire coursed through me, making my head spin and trapping my words in my throat as he slipped his fingers in and out of my core in a torturous rhythm. His thumb rubbed against my clit in firm, gentle circles. I could feel the heat building up inside me, threatening to burst and spill down my legs. I grabbed his wrist, trying to slow him down, but he kept his rhythm, his breaths ragged and strained.

"Answer me, Elodie." He demanded. I opened my eyes and the wild, barely tamed desire in his nearly sent me over the edge completely. I nodded, unable to find the words while the heat continued to build.

"Say it. Let me hear it."

"It's all for you." I moaned. Mekhi nodded and picked up the speed of his fingers. My legs shook. I was dangerously close to cumming all over his hand. With his free hand, he covered my mouth just as the orgasm ripped through my entire body. Fire blazed behind his eyes as I sunk my teeth into his hand, moaning wildly.

As the last waves of the orgasm rocked through me, Mekhi spun me around. Before I knew what was happening, I was leaning against the piano while he kneeled in front of me and snatched my bottoms and panties down to my ankles in one fell swoop. I stepped out of them, widening my stance in front of him. He paused a moment to take in the sight of me half naked and vulnerable in front of him. His eyes roamed over every part of my body.

"More beautiful than I imagined." He whispered, meeting my gaze. "I bet you taste just as good."

My head rolled back to rest against the piano while he planted gentle kisses up my thighs and gripped my butt with both hands, his fingers still wet from being inside me. I couldn't believe we were doing this. When he invited me over, I hadn't planned to be in his piano room with my ankles on his shoulders. But I'll definitely say it was a pleasant surprise.

I inhaled sharply when his tongue pressed against my core, lapping up every drop of me. His eyes closed and a deep, animalistic growl rattled low in his throat.

"You taste incredible." He groaned. He used his fingers to spread me open wider so he could get deeper. I felt that familiar heat building up again as he sucked gently on my clit, groaning in pleasure while he swallowed up everything I had to offer. My eyes rolled into the back of my head as a second orgasm spilled out of me. He knew exactly what to do to drive me wild, and all I wanted was to feel him inside me. All of him. I reached down, placed a hand under his chin, and pulled. He lifted his head, chin dripping with the evidence of my orgasm.

I leaned forward to kiss his lips, tasting myself on them. I had never done that before. I had no idea what came over me, but this man unlocked something animalistic from deep inside me. Something feral and untamed. He stood in front of me, gazing down at me with an expression full of emotion. More than I expected to see in a moment like this. Without a word, I grabbed the waistband of his sweatpants in both hands and pulled. He watched me, licking the last of my juices off of his lips.

"Talk to me," he said finally. "Tell me what you want." Him being so demanding sexually was turning me on almost as much as seeing the look in his eyes.

"I want you."

12

Mekhi

I want you. Three simple words unraveled me faster than I thought possible. Before I could respond or make a move, she pulled down my sweatpants and pulled out my dick. It sprang free, eager to be shown attention. Her eyes widened slightly before she grabbed the base with one hand and swirled her tongue around the tip.

"Jesus, Elodie," I hissed, gritting my teeth. Her soft lips against my dick were almost too much to handle. I focused on the wall behind me, determined not to let myself cum too soon. Not when I wanted to make this moment last as long as I could. She slipped me further into her warm mouth. The sensation made my toes curl in my socks. I had been dreaming of this moment ever since I saw her for the first time at the school. Something about her had drawn me in and led me to this moment and now that we were here, and I didn't want it to end.

I knew if she kept sucking me like this, I wouldn't last much longer. "Stand up." My voice came out ragged and hoarse, but I didn't care. When she stood up, I instructed her to sit on the piano bench in front of me. When she did, I grabbed her thighs and pulled her forward. Her back thwacked against the middle C and for some reason, that made me even more ready to see what she felt like wrapped around my dick. Her pretty, pink center sat open and waiting for me. I grabbed my dick and slid it inside, inch by inch. She tilted her head back with a moan and closed her eyes.

The sound of her pleasure was music to my ears. It was already my new favorite song. I pulled out painfully slowly and then pushed back inside of her. My muscles tensed with each thrust while Elodie's beautiful face twisted in pleasure. I could watch her like this all day- breasts bouncing and hair draping over the piano keys while I slammed in and out of her. I would see this in my dreams later, playing it over and over in my head until I memorized every note of her orgasms, every tone of her pleasure.

She placed a hand against my stomach and pushed lightly. She wanted me to ease back a little. She tried and failed to scoot back, the piano, digging further into her back and pressing a few random notes.

"Don't run from it, baby. Take this dick. Take all of it. I know you can do it. Can you do that for me?" I grunted, continuing my strokes. Elodie nodded, completely breathless and spent. I watched her with her head back and her mouth open in pure ecstasy. I could feel the pressure building inside me. I wouldn't last much longer. Not in her, not like this.

"Mekhi," she whimpered, "Please. I need more." She grasped at my thighs, trying to bring me in closer. It was enough to drive me crazy. I grabbed her waist and thrusted wildly, feeling that familiar tension building at a rapid pace. She leaned up to kiss me, shoving her tongue in my mouth and sending me careening over the edge with a low growl, my mind already daydreaming about the next time we could do it again.

A sharp knock on the door made me freeze mid-daydream, followed by a small voice. Kellan. In the heat of the moment, we had both forgotten he was here and waiting for us to decorate the tree.

"What are you guys doing in there? You've been in there forever!" He whined.

"Go get everything set up and we'll be out soon!" I called, struggling to sound normal. There was a pause before the sound of his footsteps could be heard heading back down the hallway. I turned to Elodie to see her eyes wide with a hand over her mouth.

"Oh, my God!" she hissed. "We forgot about Kellan!"

"In my defense, I didn't expect to be accosted like this." I laughed, planting soft kisses down her neck. She smacked my chest and even though I was sad to have to leave this moment with her, I was still so grateful it happened.

"I didn't hear any complaints." Elodie grinned, grabbing her panties and pajama bottoms from where I had tossed them earlier. I grabbed her chin and placed a soft kiss on her lips.

"No complaints from me." We both took turns freshening up in the bathroom before heading back out to the living room. Kellan had arranged the ornaments by color and shape. I felt a wave of guilt wash over me. We really had been in there for a while.

"Are you guys ready now?" he demanded, folding his arms across his chest.

"My fault. We were um..." I searched for an excuse. "I was showing Elodie a song I could play."

I heard her snort behind me. Kellan narrowed his eyes at both of us. I kept my face neutral even though I desperately wanted to laugh at the angry expression he was wearing. It didn't help he was tapping his foot impatiently like an angry old man. After a moment of him trying to stare us down, he shrugged and pointed to the piles of ornaments.

"I put them in groups based on the color and the shape."

"What's the color scheme going to be?" Elodie asked, stepping from behind me and observing the ornaments. He tilted his head and stared at her.

"Color scheme?"

Elodie threw her hands up in mock frustration. "Of course! You have to have a theme! Otherwise, you'll just be covering the tree in all sorts of mess with no structure. We need structure."

"I like blue." He said, after taking the time to look at each stack of ornaments. Elodie nodded and placed a hand on her chin, a serious look of contemplation on her face. Kellan stared at her, waiting for her to make her choice.

"I think I'm going to go with gold. What about you?" They both turned to me expectantly. I froze. Hadn't realized that I would be expected to pick a color. I had figured we'd just use them all until the tree was decorated. I should have known this would be a much bigger deal, but at the moment all I could think about was taking Elodie back into the room and making her scream my-

"Mekhi?" Elodie asked. I blinked, surprised. The two of them stared at me; Kellan looked confused and Elodie with a knowing smirk.

"Silver," I said, with a shrug. I honestly didn't care what color the tree was. As long as they were happy with it, I would be more than satisfied.

"There we go. I think we're finally finished." Elodie placed her hands on her hips and smiled proudly. My entire house looked like something out of a Pinterest Christmas post. Garland and string lights on the doorways, figurines on the mantle and the counter of the pass through, a glittery centerpiece that Elodie has fashioned out of the extra ornaments and some pinecones from outside sat in the middle of the dining room table.

My mother would be proud of the amount of decorating that had been done. No corner of the living room, dining room, or kitchen had been left untouched by the glitter and the nonsense of the holiday. I thought my mom had been an elf, but nothing had topped Elodie's enthusiasm for the season. Even Kellan had given up midway through and fallen asleep on the couch while he waited for her to finish.

"What do you think?" she asked, turning to me.

"More beautiful than I imagined," I said, echoing my sentiments from earlier. Her cheeks flushed slightly when she recognized my words. While she flitted around the house, placing ornaments in every nook and cranny, I had been thinking about the next time I could have her ankles behind my head again. After having tasted her, I knew I wouldn't be able to get enough. My body craved her like the next hit of a drug I'd become addicted to after one pull.

Kellan slept peacefully on the couch, blissfully unaware of

how hard I was falling for the woman standing in the middle of my dining room sweeping up stray bits of garland. I don't think she realized it either. Maybe she thought of earlier as a one-time thing or as scratching an itch. I'm not immature enough to not consider that as a possibility. I had been in a few of those situations myself, but in my eyes, this was something different. This was rare and beautiful; a once in a lifetime situation I had no intention of taking for granted.

"Elodie, sweetheart." I began, gently grabbing the broom from her hand. She looked up at me, waiting for me to continue, a slight smile on her face. "About earlier."

"I know. It was quick. We'll have to fix that." She wiggled her eyebrows at me and placed her hands on my chest. I grabbed her hands and held them.

"No. I mean- well, yeah, but that's not what I wanted to talk about." The seriousness in my tone made her pause, concern all over her face.

"You regret it, don't you?" She stepped away from me in embarrassment. I shook my head quickly, not wanting her to think for even a second that I had any regrets.

"No. Not at all. I've been daydreaming about that since I saw you for the first time. What I wanted to say was that I am really starting to fall for you. And I'm hoping that wasn't just a friends-with-benefit type thing for you because that's not what it was for me."

"What was it for you?" she asked.

"It was the start of forever." It slipped out, but it felt right. It felt real. Her eyes widened in surprise. I could tell she hadn't been expecting me to say it. I honestly hadn't been expecting it either, but now that it was out there, I didn't want to take it back.

"Oh wow. This is... unexpected."

I nodded, feeling deflated. She wasn't ready. That's fine. Even though we had a mind-blowing moment together, she wasn't ready for something serious. That's perfectly okay. I would just have to be patient with her. She would come around eventually.

She cupped my face in her hands and tilted my head in her direction. "What I mean is... this is unexpected, because I had been feeling the same. Just wasn't sure that you were."

"How could I not?" I asked, grabbing one of her hands and kissing it. "You are perfection in human form. I wouldn't be the man I am if I let a song as beautifully written as you slip through my fingers."

She stood on her tiptoes and planted a kiss on my lips. I grabbed her around the waist and deepened the kiss. My body was hungry for her again, as if we hadn't just explored each other earlier. My growing erection pressed against her thigh; she laughed into the kiss and pulled away.

"Control yourself!" She giggled.

"Just being near you makes my body respond. You have no idea."

"I see that," she grinned, looking pointedly down at my pants, where my dick hardened once again. I laughed.

"This is your fault, anyway. You started this."

I watched hungrily as she sauntered towards me and stood on her tip toes, bringing her face closer to mine. I leaned down, letting my lips touch her softly, enjoying each kiss from her like it was the first.

My phone buzzing on the table snapped us both out of the sex-induced trance we had been in. For a moment, I had forgotten that anyone existed outside of the two of us. The phone continued to buzz, the force of the vibrations causing it to shift around on the table. I reached for it, confused about who would call me around this time. When I saw the name on the phone, my heart dropped to my knees. It was a call from Jillian. I stared at the phone in my hand, tempted to let the phone go to voicemail.

"Hello?" I answered, warily. Elodie noticed my shift in tone. I smiled at her, trying my best to offer reassurance, even though I knew in my gut that this would be a phone call I didn't want to have right now.

"Mekhi! Hey!" Jillian's voice was pleasant, but her tone was clipped. I heard rustling in the background, meaning she was sorting through a stack of papers, most likely sitting in her home office. The job never slept, even during the holiday season.

"Hey Jill, what's up?"

"I've got really good news! We've found a placement for Kellan. I had been certain we wouldn't be able to find anyone to take him over the holidays, but we're in luck! I found a good family that has room for him." My heart cracked into a thousand pieces in my chest. I glanced over at Kellan, still sleeping peacefully on the couch with Bark Twain curled in a ball next to him. He'd only been with me for a short time, but I already couldn't imagine my home without him. He had brightened up the place in so many different ways.

"Oh. Did you tell them he could stay with me until the holiday season is finished? I'm completely fine with it."

"I did, but they're super excited to get things ready for him. The sooner the better so he can adjust to his new school and new environment." My eyes widened, which made Elodie place a hand on my arm, concern all over her face. She couldn't hear the conversation, but I had told her who Jillian was, so I'm sure she knew what was happening.

"Wait, you're transferring him out of Astoria Middle?" I asked, lowering my voice so I wouldn't wake Kellan up. The last thing I wanted was for him to hear me talking to Jillian after we'd had such a good time decorating the tree. The poor kid had been so excited to finally be in a house with a Christmas tree. He had been doing good in school while being here with me. He had a math test recently and even though he had been struggling before, he was really starting to grasp the concepts.

Taking him out of a familiar home environment and out of school, away from his friends, would absolutely crush his spirits. I'd seen it happen so many times with kids in the system. It had happened to me before my parents adopted my brother and me. I didn't want that for Kellan. I wanted him to have stability and to know where he would lay his head at the end of the day. It would also make it that much harder for me to make sure he was still doing okay.

If he was with someone local, I could at least check in on him during the school days and maybe sometimes on the weekends, just to make sure he knew he still had my support. To snatch him away from everything and everyone he'd grown familiar with seemed cruel.

"Yeah, it's a family in the next town over. Still a part of the same county, but he'll be in a newer part of the district." She paused. "You don't sound thrilled. I thought you would be excited to have your place back to yourself again."

I shot another look in Kellan's direction, worried that the conversation had somehow woken him up. I motioned to Elodie that I would be back and headed down the hallway to my bedroom for more privacy. Emotions I was unprepared for stirred around inside me.

"We've been having a great time; he's been adjusting well." I sighed.

Jillian got quiet. "You knew this would be temporary, though, Khi. It always is," she said gently.

She was right. It was literally in the title. Temporary Foster. I wasn't supposed to get attached to anyone who spent time here, but I couldn't help growing fond of Kellan. He was such a smart kid with a spirit that fought to be positive, even in the midst of everything he had been through.

"I know and you're right, but-" My voice was gruff as I struggled to reign in the emotions that were flooding through me. "When will you come get him?" I asked, absolutely dreading her answer.

"I'll come pick him up at the end of next week."

13

Elodie

Dear Diary

Elodie and Mekhi had finally crossed that line between friendship and something more It had happened after he invited her to come decorate the tree when the lingering looks and small touches built into a moment that felt inevitable

As they pulled back and their eyes met Elodie felt a rush of relief and happiness that was almost dizzying They didn t need to speak to know that everything had changed Finally they were done dancing around their feelings and they both knew this was the start of something real

"You *slept* with him?!" It was the next morning; I was getting ready for work and called an emergency Facetime chat with my girls. All five of us were going through our morning routines as I filled them in on the unexpected events of last night. I failed to mention that the journal had an extra journal entry written, waiting for me to read when I walked in the door last night. That part I saved for myself.

I smiled sheepishly and nodded at the screen. "I didn't plan to! It just happened."

I hadn't expected to be laying on his piano bench with my most vulnerable body parts exposed, but things just naturally progressed in that direction, and I didn't feel guilty about it at all. As a matter of fact, I was counting down the days until it would happen again. Crossing that milestone with Mekhi had unlocked a completely different side of him. He had already been attentive, but now he had kicked things up a notch.

"How was it?" Deja asked, pausing her makeup to give me a look. I pressed my lips together, trying and failing to suppress a smile. She let out an excited squeal and clapped her hands. Excess powder from the brush she was holding sprinkled in the air in front of her face.

"I knew it! From what I've seen, that man looks like he packs quite the punch." She wiggled her eyebrows salaciously. "If you know what I mean."

"You've met him already?" Audrey gasped, pausing tying her locs to shoot me an offended glare. "She hasn't introduced us yet."

"Relax mama bear, I haven't met him. I looked him up on Facebook." She giggled.

"Deja! You creep!" I laughed, rolling my eyes. She shrugged and went back to her makeup. I leaned forward in the mirror to put on my Christmas tree earrings that matched my green sweater and red dress pants. Sometimes I surprised even myself with the amount of Christmassy ensemble combinations I could create with my wardrobe. A talent that hasn't been used to its fullest potential.

"How did the first rehearsal with the kids go?" Brina asked. She looked crisp and professional in her perfectly tailored navy suit and minimal makeup. Sometimes I couldn't believe she was the same person twerking to the City Girls the last time we all hung out together.

"It went as well as to be expected. We've only got about four more rehearsals until we have to perform."

"Is that enough time?" Monae, who had been quiet for most of the conversation, piped up. I shrugged, grabbing my keys off the keyring nearest my front door before I left.

"I honestly don't know, but at this point, I'm not about to stress myself out over it." A chorus of 'mhms' and 'I know that's right' echoed throughout my friend group while I settled into my car, ready to begin another day of teaching. It had been a little while since I'd been able to focus on my novel and the urge to write was eating at me. I couldn't wait to get to my free period so I could hammer out a few more pages of the story.

By the time I'd made it to the school, I had a little time left to spare before the students started arriving. I spotted Mekhi's familiar black truck and smiled to myself. My heart pounded at the thought of seeing him again. His mood had been a little tense after being on the phone with Jillian, even though he still hadn't shared the specifics of the conversation. I was sure it had something to do with Kellan.

I hoped everything was okay. I unlocked my classroom and placed my things on my desk. My lessons for today were already completed. We would continue the discussion on "Roll of Thunder Hear My Cry" by Mildred D. Taylor. It was currently banned in Astoria Middle, and I was risking my career as a teacher by including it in my lessons, but I couldn't sit by while some of the most brutally honest and vulnerable stories were stomped out by the powers that be. I'd gotten more than a few angry calls from parents and ended up offering a less sensitive book as a second option, but most of my students opted to read the book, anyway. I was more fortunate enough to have a group that wanted to connect with others, not just do the assignments and then go home.

"How do you do that?" Mekhi's velvety voice rumbled from my doorway. My entire body throbbed at the sound of him being so close. I turned, struggling to keep myself under control. He stood, leaning against the doorjamb, looking good enough to eat in an olive-green monochromatic outfit. Dark olive pants with a sweater in a lighter shade. When our eyes met, he smiled at me.

"How do I do what?" I asked, suddenly feeling breathless.

He pushed off the door frame and stepped further into the room, sending a whiff of his cologne in my direction. "How do you look so beautiful just sitting here looking at your computer screen?"

It was an incredibly cheesy thing to say, but I grinned all the same. I pushed out from my desk just as he stepped even closer and wrapped my arms around his waist. His woodsy scent filled my nose, making his hug even more intoxicating. He planted a kiss on my forehead and glanced at my screen.

"Roll of Thunder?" he asked, raising an eyebrow.

"Yeah. Have you read it?"

"Of course. I thought it was recently put on the banned list, though."

I kissed his lips before turning back to my screen and getting the lesson prepared to pull up on the screen projector. "It is banned, but that doesn't mean it won't still be taught in this classroom."

"Yes, ma'am." He replied, snaking his arms back around my waist. I glanced at the clock on the wall and groaned. The kids would start showing up soon and he was stirring up things he shouldn't.

"Where's Kellan?" I asked, desperate for a distraction.

"He's in my classroom waiting for the first bell to ring."

"By the way, what was that conversation with Jillian about? You never told me. Everything okay?" Mekhi's posture stiffened at my question, and he let out a heavy sigh, running a tired hand over his beard.

"She mentioned she had a placement for him."

"That's a good thing, right?" I was confused by his sullen tone. The purpose of having Kellan stay was so he could find a permanent place to go. A family being willing to take him during the holiday season seemed like a positive, yet Mekhi stood here in front of me looking like someone had kicked his puppy.

"Sure. I guess. I'd been growing used to having him with me, though." He gave me a sheepish grin and stuffed his hands in his pockets.

"I can tell he's enjoyed staying with you. What did he say when you told him?" I busied myself with the projector remote. I could hear some of the early arrivals milling around in the hallways, heading to the cafeteria for breakfast.

Mekhi shook his head, "I haven't."

I stopped fidgeting with the remote and turned my full attention to him. He wouldn't meet my gaze, choosing instead to stare at a random tile on the floor. I waited, hoping he would follow up his statement with a promise to tell him soon, but he remained silent.

"What do you mean you haven't?"

"I haven't told him."

"Why?"

"She's moving him out of this school. Same county, different school. The family lives in the next town over." When he looked up at me, his eyes shone with unshed tears. "I can't break his heart like that, Elodie. Not now."

"You have to tell him. You can't blindside him with this. That's not right."

In my head, it made perfect sense to tell him now and give him time to process. It seemed cruel to have him walking around thinking nothing was wrong when things were getting ready to drastically change. He would need time to say goodbye to the friends he had made and to pack his things. Having been in the situation himself, Mekhi knew firsthand how hard it was. It was cruel not to give him that time.

"Look, you don't get it. He's finally having a good time after everything he's been through recently."

"He can still have a good time in his new placement."

"You don't know that. Until you've been there, you couldn't possibly know what it's like to be uprooted from everything you've grown accustomed to. I'm protecting him until I can figure something out."

"Figure what out, Mekhi? You're thinking about yourself in this moment, and not Kellan. He's a resilient kid. He can handle-"

"He shouldn't have to!" His voice was harsh; angry.

"I don't know what kind of feelings this is stirring up for you, but it's not fair to Kellan. Someone needs to put him first!" This is not how I had expected our conversation to go the day after we'd had sex for the first time and proclaimed some serious feelings for each other. I'd expected cuddling or sneaking kisses before the kids arrived, not us shouting at each other in terrible stage whispers. I didn't want to argue with him, not right before the workday started, and we wouldn't be able to see much of each other until after school.

"As if I haven't been doing that this entire time? I was the one that took him in!" Mekhi snapped, glaring at me. My heart sank. I opened my mouth to respond, but was interrupted by a loud whoop from a group of kids entering the classroom at the worst possible time. I wanted to tell them to leave and give us a little more time, but I knew I couldn't. We had to get the day started.

"Good morning, Ms. Banks! Hey Mr. D!" Sincere, one of my students called out, oblivious to the tense conversation we were just having. He tossed his bookbag next to his seat and slid into the chair. Leaning forward, with both hands gripping the desk, he squinted at the projector on the board.

"Roll of Thunder- oh shoot! We're doing that today? I thought you said that was next week." He groaned.

"I said that last week." I sighed, shaking my head at him. He shrugged at me and turned to the group of students that had walked in with them. Just like that, Mekhi and I were no longer of interest to the students. I turned back to him, hoping to finish the conversation, but the look on his face told me he wasn't in the mood to keep talking. Mekhi swallowed and nodded at the kids with a strained smile.

"You have a good day, Ms. Banks." I watched as he tapped his knuckles against my desk once and left the classroom without so much as a backwards glance.

I felt bad. No, not just bad. I felt terrible. Mekhi had pretty much avoided me for the rest of the day. I wasn't even able to catch him during our lunch break, which tells me he was working hard to make himself scarce. During practice, he had been quiet and withdrawn. Even the students noticed the difference.

As soon as everything had ended, he grabbed his things and left before I could get to him. I sighed, watching him walk brusquely to his car with Kellan following beside him, talking a mile a minute. Alex hovered nearby, watching me watch Mekhi and Kellan leave.

"Are you alright?" he asked. I nodded, blinking back the tears that were pushing at the corners of my eyes. Mekhi would come around. He just needed a minute to process things, however my heart broke for Kellan. Watching him laugh with his friends during practice, looking like the carefree child he deserved to be, I understood a little about why Mekhi didn't want to break the news to him. I wouldn't want to be the one responsible for wiping that smile off his face, either.

"You know he's leaving, right?" Alex's voice interrupted my thoughts again.

I glanced up at him confused, "Who?"

"Your boyfriend." The disapproval in his tone was palpable. "He's leaving at the end of the Christmas season. I heard it from the science teacher. He's got some fancy music gig coming up."

"Okay. What's your point?"

"You should be with someone who won't leave you behind." Alex nodded at Mekhi's retreating form, a smug smile on his face.

"Alex, please let this go. You and I are friends. Nothing more." I folded my arms and glared at him, irritated he was still holding on to the idea of us. We were long over. We went out once, and that was enough for me to decide that I wasn't interested. As soon as Mekhi entered the picture, there was no hope for anyone else.

"Well, no, I mean- of course I know that I'm just saying that-"

"Have a good night, Alex." Without waiting for him to respond, I grabbed my things and headed out to my car. I pulled out my phone and called my grandma, needing to vent to someone who would understand. As soon as her gentle voice filled my ears, I sobbed.

"Hello sweet child," she greeted me. I could hear the smile in her voice.

"Grandmada." I choked out. "I think I messed up."

"I'm sure it's nothing a cup of hot cocoa can't fix. Come. I'll have some ready when you get here."

True to her word, there was a steaming hot cup of cocoa waiting for me when I entered my grandmother's kitchen. Her curly hair was tucked neatly into her purple satin bonnet, and her matching house coat was pulled snugly around her body. She waited patiently while I took a small sip and then another. We sat like that for a moment, in complete silence. Every time I opened my mouth to speak, my heart squeezed in my chest and the tears threatened to spill over again.

"Did I ever tell you about when your grandfather asked me to marry him?" she asked finally. I picked my head up and looked at her. She was staring down into her cup of cocoa, her hands wrapped tightly around the mug.

"No. I don't think so." I sniffed.

"I was so mad at him that day." she smiled wistfully. "He had forgotten me at the airport."

I threw my head back and laughed. "What? There's no way!"

"Oh yes. In his defense, my flight had gotten canceled, and I'd had to catch a different one, so I was a bit earlier than he'd planned. He was running around that day, planning the perfect surprise for me to come home to that he had completely forgotten the time."

"How long were you there?" I asked, leaning forward. She threw a look at me and pursed her lips.

"Six hours! And I had run out of quarters for the pay phone. By the time he remembered, it was dark outside, and I had completely sweated out my hair." She lifted the cup to her lips, blew the steam, and then took a sip. I watched, mesmerized by her graceful movements. It was hard to imagine her in public with unmanageable hair.

"Did he apologize?" I asked, take a drink from my mug. The milk chocolaty taste slid down my throat like velvet, warming me up on the inside.

"Of course. He spent the entire way back from the airport begging my forgiveness."

"I bet you gave him a hard time, didn't you?"

"You'd better believe it!" We both laughed at the memory. She turned to me, her eyes shining with tears. "But when we got home, there was an entire scene waiting for me. It was like a movie. Rose petals and candles all over the place."

She reached out and stroked my hair, getting lost in the memory as she told it. "He was so nervous his entire body was shaking, but he got on one knee and asked me to be his wife. Told me it was the start of our forever." My heart thudded at her words, remembering Mekhi saying something similar the other day about the two of us. Granted, we were still riding on the high of mind-blowing sex, but it still felt genuine.

"I'm scared I ruined things, Grandmada." I whispered, unable to look her in the eyes. "You gave me the journal, and it told me about Mekhi, but then I ruined it. Like I ruin everything."

"I don't believe that."

"I said something stupid, and I hurt his feelings. I'm not sure if he's going to want to talk to me anymore!" Laying my head on my arm, I let out the tears I had been stifling with a desperate wail.

"That's the thing about real love, sweetheart. It's more resilient than that. Men are sensitive creatures. More sensitive than we give them credit for. Just give him time. He'll come back around." She slid off her stool and wrapped her arms around me in a comforting hug. I sunk into her embrace, praying what she said was true.

Hopefully, he will come around soon.

14

Mekhi

"What's wrong?" Kellan asked, searching my face. We just ordered pizza and were watching a movie while the Christmas lights twinkled behind us. Well, Kellan had been watching the movie. I spent most of it staring blankly at the television. Everything in this house now reminded me of Elodie, from the hideous reindeer figurines on the mantle above the fireplace to the haphazardly glued centerpiece in the middle of the dining room table.

"Nothing, kid. I'm fine." I said half-heartedly. Kellan narrowed his eyes at me and then snatched the remote from where it sat on the coffee table and turned off the television.

"That's bull!" He shouted. I glanced at him, shocked. The look on my face caused him to deflate a little, but he held my gaze in an impressive show of bravery. "Did Ms. Elodie say something mean? You have been walking around looking like someone peed in your cereal!"

I chuckled, "We aren't seeing eye to eye right now, but we'll be fine."

I watched as his face changed slightly, a look of panic washing over his features. "Is it me? Did I do something?"

"No. Of course not. Why would you think that?"

"You haven't really talked to me all day. I thought I made you mad." Kellan hung his head. I sighed, feeling like an absolute douchebag for making him feel like he caused my foul mood. Truth is, I've been struggling with telling him about his new placement. Elodie's words echoed in my head throughout the day. So much so that I could barely focus on the lesson. The kids ended up playing around on their instruments, one student impressing his friends by being able to play Cardi B's "Money" on the piano. Elodie was right, and I knew it, but my ego wouldn't let me admit I was being selfish.

"We have to talk, man to man." Kellan swallowed nervously, but nodded, making his expression blank. The same way I used to when I was expected to have those hard conversations as a kid.

"I had a conversation with Jillian," I began, searching his face for any signs. He stared at me, offering nothing. "She found a placement for you."

I stayed quiet, allowing him time to turn my words over in his mind. He chewed on his bottom lip, his brows pulling together in confusion. "I thought I would get to stay here?"

"No, being here with me was only supposed to be temporary." I tried to keep my voice even and my tone as gentle as I could, even though my emotions were threatening to spill out. Kellan stared at me, his eyes growing glassy. I looked away, unable to stomach the look of hurt on his face.

"You don't want me?" His voice was barely audible.

"Kellan, don't think that way. This is your opportunity to have a family and-"

"But I wanted you to be my family!" he interrupted. His voice cracked at the end of the sentence, making my heart crack with it. I opened my mouth, not even sure what to say, just desperate to comfort him somehow. Everything I thought to tell him at that moment didn't seem like enough.

"You'll have so many opportunities with this new family. You'll have a sister and the school you'll be going to has a really good music program. You'll be fine." Neither one of us believed my words. Kellan's shoulders slouched. He carried the weight of the world on his twelve-year-old shoulders, and I already knew that there wasn't anything I could say to make that better.

"I'll visit you whenever I can." I tried anyway. "We can still figure out some time for your piano lessons. You've been getting really good. We don't want that to stop, right?"

"Can I be excused?" His voice was flat and emotionless, even though fresh tears slipped down his cheeks.

"What about your dinner?" I motioned to the slice of pizza he had left half eaten on his plate. He shook his head. I didn't bother to stop him as he walked quickly down the hallway and to his room, the door clicking shut behind him a moment later. I let out a deep breath. The Christmas tree twinkled and sparkled, taunting me with every flash of light. I had just known he would be with me until the end of the holidays. I hadn't even bothered to consider a family taking him before then.

My emotions felt like a tangled mess. I wanted him to have the best chance, and from what Jillian had told me, this family was very well-off and resourceful. He would have access to things other children, especially children of color, could only dream about. Jillian had gushed about how they had plans to enroll him in music lessons from teachers even more credentialed and experienced than I was. I should be happy. I should be absolutely over the moon that I was able to provide a place where he felt safe enough until his permanent placement was secured.

Instead, I felt like someone had cracked open my chest and was digging their fingernails into my heart. I pulled out my phone without thinking and called my little brother. In moments like these, he always knew what to say to provide clarity. He picked up quickly.

"Give me a minute sweetheart," he said to someone in the background, "Yo, Khi. You good?"

"Am I interrupting?" I asked, raising an eyebrow. I honestly wasn't surprised. Montrell was nothing if not a ladies' man. Rarely had I seen him without some type of dealings with a woman.

"Honestly, yes. So, what's up?"

"My bad bro, I just-" I sighed, "I'm feeling a bit lost."

There was a shuffling noise and then the soft click of a door. I guess he had left the room for more privacy. I leaned forward in my chair, placing my head in my hand.

"Talk to me," Montrell said.

"It's Kellan. They found a placement for him."

"That's a good thing, right?" he asked.

"Yes."

"Then why do you sound like that?" His question was met with silence. "Ah. You wanted him to stay."

Hearing my brother say the words I had been trying not to admit to myself landed like a punch to the gut. I did want him to stay. Even though he had such an excellent opportunity in front of him, part of me had been hoping Jillian would struggle trying to find a place for him, and he'd be able to just stay with me.

"Yeah. Yeah, I guess I did. I prolonged the conversation with him because my admitting it out loud meant that it was real. I didn't want it to be real."

"You know how this works, though, Khi. We've both been through it."

"I know, man, I just didn't expect-" I paused, turning to look at all the Christmas decorations. The glitter and the garland, and the ornaments of every color and shape. My house had so quickly turned into a home not just because of Elodie, but because of Kellan. When I opened my home to him, it had been just to help a friend. I hadn't expected him to add so much to my life so soon.

"Look, genuine family is hard to find. It's not always blood. Family are the people that wake up every day and choose you. I've learned that when you find those people, you need to hold on to them. As hard as you can."

I nodded, even though I knew Montrell couldn't see me. He was right. Family is hard to find. He and I had been so fortunate to be kept together, so many stories had ended differently for other kids in the system.

"Yeah, you're right." I sighed.

Montrell chuckled. "This is nothing new. By the way, now that I got you on the phone, we going half on mom's Christmas present this year, right?"

"Nah, man. You're just saying that so you can mooch off whatever my gift is."

"She's so hard to buy for!" He groaned. I laughed at him, feeling lighter for the first time today.

"Thanks for talking to me real quick. I'll let you get back to whoever- I mean whatever you're doing."

"Funny. Should have sent you to voicemail." He quipped and hung up before I could respond. I shook my head and tossed my phone on the couch while I cleaned up the pizza. I could hear Kellan in his room, watching videos on his phone. I'd give him a little more time and then go check on him.

While I straightened up, my mind drifted back to Elodie. She and I hadn't had the chance to finish our conversation earlier and the way we had left things left a bad taste in my mouth. It was my fault for the way it ended. I had been too in my feelings to really hear what she was saying. Before I talked myself out of it, I grabbed my phone and dialed her number.

"Hello?" Her voice was uncertain.

"Hey. Do you have time to stop by so we can talk?" I asked.

She breathed out a sigh of relief, "Oh, thank God."

"What?"

"I'm outside. I brought Christmas cookies as a peace offering."

Surprised, I threw open my front door to see her standing there holding a Walmart bag with a silly grin on her face. Without a word, I pressed the call end button and then scooped her up into my arms. She was warm and smelled like minty chocolate. I chuckled to myself, completely unsurprised that she would make her perfume Christmas-themed as well.

"I'm so sorry." She whispered into my neck. Confused, I pulled away to look at her face. Her eyes were glassy, like she was trying not to cry.

"Wait, why are you sorry?" I asked.

"For what I said earlier. I was insensitive and I hurt you. I'm so sorry."

"You were right. I wasn't being fair to Kellan. I didn't want him to have to leave so soon. I figured if I put off telling him, I could pretend that it didn't exist." I gently took the grocery bag from her and glanced in, laughing at the different kinds of cookies shoved into one bag. "Did you leave any at the store?"

"I wanted to make sure I got what everyone liked." She shrugged. "Where's Kellan?"

"He's in his room. I told him."

Her eyes widened. "I'm guessing he didn't take it well?" I

shook my head and ran a hand over my beard.

"It wasn't a pleasant conversation; his words mixed with the look of pure heartbreak on his face keep playing on a loop in my head."

"Get the cookies ready to bake. I'll go talk to him."

I had just placed the last of the cookie dough on a baking sheet when I felt tiny arms wrap around my waist. I turned just in time to see Kellan peek from under my arm.

"Hey. You good?" I asked, suppressing a smile.

He nodded. "I'm sorry I was mad at you. I just really like it here."

"I enjoyed having you," I replied. Elodie watched us from the doorway, a small content smile on her lips. I looked up at her and mouthed 'thank you'. I had no idea what she had said to him, but whatever it was had brought him out of his room. He probably would have been stuck in there for the rest of the night had she not intervened. Her smile widened, and she nodded, before pushing herself off the doorframe and moving towards us.

"Alright. Who's ready for Christmas cookies?" she asked, clapping her hands together excitedly. I stepped out of the way so she could place the baking sheets into the already preheated oven. "We need Christmas tunes!"

Kellan and I both groaned. "As long as it's not All I Want for Christmas!"

She whirled around from where she was busily pulling up a playlist on Spotify and huffed, "That is a classic Christmas song. Next, you're going to tell me you don't want to hear Let it Snow."

"We don't." Kellan shrugged and then squealed with laughter as Elodie charged at him, threatening to tickle him until he changed his mind.

"Fine. Since you two Scrooges don't want to hear two of the best and blackest Christmas songs, then tell me, what do you want to hear?" She pulled up her phone, ready to type in the names of the songs we suggested on Spotify.

"You're a Mean One!" Kellan shouted. Elodie glanced up at me and then laughed. His fascination with the song still made no sense to me. It wasn't even one of the newer versions. He preferred the deep-voiced Thurl Ravenscroft version. It's the first song he would request whenever I asked what song he wanted to listen to. I'd heard it more times over these few weeks than I have in most of my life.

Soon the house smelled like cookies and the woman of my dreams danced around, pretending to be the Grinch with the twelve-year-old boy who had changed my life in such a short period. Watching them, I knew it didn't want to end. I couldn't let it. I wanted this right here, during every holiday and every season, not just Christmas. I wanted to see these two on birthdays and Easter. I wanted to make cookies on Valentine's Day and wear green on St. Patrick's Day.

I wanted my own ugly Christmas sweaters to match Elodie's seemingly endless collections. I wanted to be the one to see Kellan go off to high school and then college. I wanted to be the reason he no longer had to question where he would sleep at night.

I wanted to be the one to give him what my parents had given my brother and me. I wanted this. I wanted these two. I needed them. Permanently. While the two of them busied themselves with taking the cookies out of the oven, I grabbed my phone and stepped out of the room. I took a deep breath and dialed the number, feeling even more sure of my decision with each ring of the phone.

"Hello? Everything okay?" Jillian seemed obviously surprised to hear from me.

"Cancel it," I said quickly. The line went quiet for a moment.

"Cancel it?" she asked. "Cancel what?"

"The foster family. Tell them no. Tell them we're sorry, but things have changed." My words were rushed as excitement coursed through me. It made so much sense I didn't know why it didn't click for me earlier. It should have been my first option when Jillian had called me, telling me there was a family that was interested in taking Kellan away from everything he had grown accustomed to. I should have said it when I realized that waking up one day and not seeing him sleeping curled up in a ball in the guest bedroom would break my heart into a thousand jagged pieces. If he didn't want this to end, then I wouldn't let it.

"What's changed?' Jillian asked, obviously not catching on to what I was saying. I glanced behind me to make sure they couldn't hear what I was saying. They were sharing cookies and talking excitedly about something, their heads close together like they were plotting something in secret. It confirmed everything for me.

"Everything. I want him to stay here with us. With me."

"Mekhi, we talked about this-"

"No. We haven't. Not this."

"I'm not understanding. What are you-" I cut her off before she could finish her question.

"I want to adopt Kellan."

15

Elodie

"Okay. So, make sure you read pages thirty-six through forty-nine. There will be a quiz on it Monday!" I called out as my students shoved their way out of the classroom. It was the day of the musical and even though we were more than prepared and had run through the entire program countless times, I was still nervous.

It reminded me of those times when I was a kid, and it was almost my turn to read out loud or perform in one of the many clubs and programs my mother had stuck me in. I'd be so nervous and so intent on running through my part repeatedly in my head that I would miss my cue. I was terrified this time because I was the director of the entire thing. The kids were counting on me to make them look good in front of their parents, friends, and whoever else they had invited.

"You ready for tonight?" At the sound of Mekhi's voice, my tense muscles instantly relaxed. As the last student filed out of the classroom and into the hallway, he stepped inside and closed the door behind him.

"I'm so nervous," I admitted, chewing on my bottom lip.

"I can take your mind off of everything for a little while." He whispered, leaning in to kiss me softly.

"Not in the school building," I hissed, absolutely mortified. He narrowed his eyes and then laughed. The sound sent another wave of calm through me.

"That's not what I meant. Get your mind out of the gutter, woman. Kellan is hanging out with a friend of his until it's time to get ready for the musical."

"Okay. We have more time to practice?" I stood from my desk, ready to pull him toward the auditorium. Mekhi shook his head and grabbed my arm to stop me, an amused smile on his face.

"No. Let's go get some fresh air. You're a ball of nervous energy and it's making me nervous too."

It was a few hours before the musical and my stomach had made its permanent home in my throat. I couldn't figure out why I wanted so badly for this musical to be successful. Maybe it was because Principal Ardell had caught wind of Mekhi and me dating and if we could make this thing go off without a hitch, then maybe she would be less annoyed or maybe it was because I couldn't stand being in front of people.

Whatever the reason for my nerves was, I could barely focus on anything else. Mekhi had tried to relax me earlier that morning while we got ready for work together, but nothing seemed to work. I kept imagining something going wrong.

"Beautiful, you have got to stop freaking out." Mekhi sauntered up behind me as I put the finishing touches on my makeup and kissed my exposed shoulder. My dress, a glittery red knee-length dress that Deja and Monae had been more than happy to pick out for me, hugged my curves in a way that made me feel sexy.

I turned to face Mekhi and blushed at the way he was letting his eyes roam over my body. "You like what you see?"

He grabbed me by the waist and pulled me closer, planting sweet kisses along my neck so he didn't mess up my makeup. He stopped when he reached my ear. "You look absolutely stunning." He whispered.

"You don't think it's too much?" I asked, feeling self-conscious. I tugged at the fabric stretching over my thighs and cursed myself for indulging in those extra cookies with Kellan and Mekhi.

"No. I think it's perfect. Tell Deja and Monae they can pick out your clothes any time they like." He fixed his tie and then smacked my butt as he left the room. "I'm going to go call Jillian to confirm the interview for tomorrow." He called over his shoulder.

After telling Jillian that he wanted to adopt Kellan, both of them had been subjected to the long and grueling process of adoption. DSS had sent over at least two social workers to do a walkthrough of the home and interviews with both Kellan and Mekhi.

Seeing how happy the two of them were filled my heart with so much joy. It was like the final piece of the puzzle clicked into place the day Kellan walked inside Mekhi's house. It made sense for him to stay.

I finished the last bit of my look for the night and headed into the living room. Mekhi stood, helping Kellan with his tie. They both wore matching black suits with red ties. I couldn't wait to see what the rest of the kids would look like. The set had been designed to look like a nativity scene and the children would be fitted with their wings and halos once we got to the school.

"You look pretty and sparkly!" Kellan said when he saw me approaching. Mekhi turned to look at me again, silently taking in every inch of my body in his smoldering gaze. I blushed and turned away from him, worried I would melt if I stared into that heat for too long.

"Thanks!" I breathed, fanning myself with my hand. "You clean up nicely, sir."

His chest puffed with pride. The two of them had spent two days after school looking for the perfect suit and tie for tonight. When Kellan had finally decided on one, Mekhi had purchased it immediately, scared he would change his mind if he had more options.

"Do you remember your speaking part?" I asked. Each of the kids had a small piece to recite between songs to keep the show moving and explain a little about which songs were chosen and why. Kellan had been feverishly practicing his speech, making sure to add emphasis in the necessary spots. He nodded proudly and tapped the side of his head.

"It's all up here. I've been practicing!"

"What about you, Mr. Davis? Do you remember all your parts?" I asked, turning to Mekhi.

He squinted at me. "You mean the music?"

"Yes."

"I remember the music, Elodie. This ain't my first rodeo." He laughed, shaking his head. He was right. I had forgotten about his experience playing as the main pianist for popular musicians in the town. His confidence eased my nerves a little, but not enough to remove the butterflies from the pit of my stomach. How do people perform constantly? Doing it this once was enough to make me want to vomit into the nearest toilet. I took a deep breath, hoping the air would further calm my frazzled nerves.

"You're right. Sorry." I smiled sheepishly and followed them out to the car.

When we arrived at the school, cars had already started filled the parking lot. I spotted Brina's SUV parked right next to Deja's Nissan and smiled to myself. I had asked my girls to come, but hadn't expected them to make it with their schedules. I'd bet Audrey and Monae were parked somewhere out here too, if they didn't catch a ride with Deja or Brina.

This would be the first time they'd seen Mekhi. I had planned to introduce him to my friend group after the musical was over. The way he looked when he leaned over the piano keys was magical to me. I couldn't wait for them to witness the same thing that made me fall for him.

Principal Ardell stepped up to the podium of the H. Tubeck Auditorium while I lined up the children backstage. Kellan threw me an excited thumbs-up as Mekhi positioned himself behind the piano. Where I felt nothing but nerves, Mekhi oozed confidence. He was in his element, performing in front of a crowd. Meanwhile, I wanted to run and hide until the show was over.

"Hello everyone. Thank you for coming. Here at Astoria Middle, we like to donate the proceeds from our Christmas play tickets to a worthy cause. This year, we have chosen to donate to Forever Families. It's a program that was started to help foster kids find permanent placements. We have children in our very own school who have been placed in the system, so this cause was very near and dear to our hearts..."

As she spoke, I looked over at Mekhi, who had been surprised by the cause chosen for this year. He locked eyes with me, realization dawning on him, and nodded stiffly with a quiet 'Thank you'. I could tell he was trying to keep his composure while in front of everyone.

"Okay! Now, without further ado, here's what you all have been waiting for! Astoria Middle Presents to you our Christmas musical!" the excited whispers from the kids as they took their places on stage died down and the curtains drew back, revealing them to the crowd. A roar of applause erupted as I took the mic from Principal Ardell and addressed the audience.

"Thank you for coming, everyone! About a month or so ago, Principal Ardell volunteered me to help with the Christmas program for this year." Giggles erupted through the auditorium. "Like I told her, luckily I love Christmas, so this was a welcome change. This has been a wonderful group of kids. I've had a great time working with them and I'm excited to show you what we've come up with!"

I turned to the kids, my eyes landing directly on a smiling Kellan. He was grinning so hard I couldn't help but smile back. "You guys ready?"

"So, you two came up with that yourselves?" Audrey asked. My girls found me after the program had ended. I scanned the crowd for Mekhi, wondering where he had gone off to. I spotted him next to a guy that looked like the lighter skinned version of him, with light eyes. Mekhi had mentioned he had a brother.

"Yeah, we did. What'd you guys think?" I asked.

"You're wasting your talent just being a teacher." Brina shook her head.

"That's what I've been telling her." Mekhi's voice surprised me. He had just been on the other side of the room talking to the guy and now they both stood next to us. "Ladies. I've heard so much about you, I'm Mekhi." He shook each of their hands.

"We've heard a lot about you too." Deja grinned devilishly. I widened my eyes at her, begging her to stay quiet. She stuck her tongue out at me and laughed.

"I bet. This is my little brother, Montrell." He nodded at the handsome man standing next to him.

"Nice to meet you, ladies." Montrell smiled at each of my friends until his eyes landed on Audrey and turned surprisingly cold. She glared back at him without responding.

"Is everyone hungry? I figured we could grab something to eat, and you ladies can pelt me with the questions I'm sure you're dying to ask." Mekhi winked at me and planted a quick kiss on the side of my head.

Brina nodded. "I do have questions. Do you have any priors, Mekhi?"

"No, I don't."

"Any baby mamas? Hidden children of any kind?" Embarrassment at my friend's probing questions washed over me, but Mekhi took it in stride. He paused for a moment, waiting to see if Brina was serious, and then laughed when he realized she was.

"Only kid I have is Kellan." Hearing him say that made me want to melt into a puddle right there. At the sound of his name, Kellan came running up from somewhere in the crowd. He wrapped his arms around my waist and squeezed.

"Did I do good?!" he asked, buzzing with excited energy. I nodded and hugged him back.

"So good! Are you hungry? We're going to grab something to eat, Mekhi's treat."

"Yesss! Can we get pizza? Or burgers? I haven't had a burger in a while!" He hopped on the balls of his feet. Mekhi watched him for a moment, then shook his head.

"Not sure where all this energy is coming from, but yes. We can get a burger. You guys interested?" He glanced up at my friends to see.

"I could eat," Monae said quietly, shrugging. Slowly, everyone else agreed, which made Kellan pump his fist in the air and let out a whoop. I wasn't sure where all that energy was coming from either, but it was infectious. I had to resist the urge to yell myself.

I was so happy the musical was over. Granted, I was so grateful that it had brought me to Mekhi, but the stress of performing in front of the entire school and their parents was enough to keep me feeling anxious for the entire week leading up to this performance. Now that it was done, I could go back to focusing on my novel. With the excitement of these last few weeks, I hadn't written a word. The novel had completely left my brain, but now the ideas were piling up, desperate to be put on the page.

"You coming?" I had been lost in my thoughts and hadn't noticed Mekhi extending his hand in my direction. He searched my face, trying to make sure I was okay. I smile at him and grab his outstretched hand.

"Of course. You guys go ahead to the car. I'll be there in a minute." Mekhi nodded and ushered a chattering Kellan out to the car. My friends and Mekhi's brother followed suit. I waited for a second to make sure they were gone and then turned to head to my classroom. The hallways were completely empty. Everyone was mostly in the auditorium. I saw the occasional parent on the way to my destination. When I'd made it to my classroom, I'd unlocked the door and stepped inside.

Everything looked exactly as I had left it earlier. I reached in my desk for the bag I had dropped off before the performance and placed it on the desk in front of me. I cracked open the bag and peeked inside, checking to see if it was still there and undisturbed. It was. Inside my purse sat the journal. I sank into my chair and opened it, flipping to the last page with writing in it. I still couldn't explain this phenomenon, but I had learned to just accept it. So far, it had done nothing but confirm what I had been suspecting from the moment Mekhi and I had talked for the very first time at the homeless shelter.

That I'd found something special in him, something that I didn't need or want to let go of. I had always wanted a love like my grandparents. Maybe this was life's way of giving me that chance. Earlier today, I'd seen it on my nightstand, pen writing furiously while I was packing my bag to come to Mekhi's house to get ready for tonight. I had wanted to stop and read it right then, but in my hurry, I hadn't had the chance to open it, so I grabbed it and shoved it in my bag for later. As I sat here in my classroom, I finally gave myself the chance to take in the words.

Dear Diary

Their connection wasn t instant fireworks it was more like a spark that grew steadily illuminating their lives in ways neither could ve predicted At first they bonded over simple moments conversations at the homeless shelter or over texts stolen glances and an unspoken understanding that made each meeting feel significant In Mekhi Elodie discovered someone who saw her not as an adventure to chase but as a partner to grow with And in Elodie Mekhi found not just excitement but a love that stirred his soul and made him believe in the magic of human connection Together they realized love wasn t about perfection or grand gestures but about being present for each other growing together and choosing one another in all their flawed beautiful humanity

Their love was the kind that felt like coming home

Epilogue
Elodie

10 Months Later

"So, it's a magical journal?" Mekhi asked, staring at me incredulously. I sighed. I knew he wasn't going to believe me, but he had found the journal in my things while he was helping me unpack and it felt weird not telling him what it was. My grandmother had warned me that people wouldn't understand or believe the power of the journal. Until it was time to give it to the next person, it was my job to protect it. It had been almost a year since my Grandmada had given me the journal as a Christmas gift.

Now, here I stood, trying to convince Mekhi that the journal was something magical. He listened intently as I explained it, but I could almost see the exact moment he stopped believing the story. His eyes glazed over, and he stopped paying as much attention, instead choosing to watch Kellan as he played basketball on the PlayStation behind us. As a thirteen-year-old, he was skillfully ignoring our conversation. Something he had perfected over his last year of being with Mekhi. The adoption process that Mekhi had started last year around this time hadn't been finalized yet, but it would be any day now. We were still waiting to hear from his social worker, Jillian, on the last necessary documents.

"Yes. You see this writing in here?" I opened it and flipped to a random page, pulling his attention back to our conversation and away from the video game. The familiar swirly script was visible for him to see. He peered at it and then looked back at me. "This looks nothing like my handwriting."

"I'll give you that. Yours is much messier than this. Ow!" He whined when I smacked him in the stomach.

"So how it works is, it tells you who to give it to next, and then that person's love story is basically written for them to see. It doesn't predict the future; it just confirms it for you. It takes the guesswork out of it."

"So, we got together because of a book?" The skepticism in his voice was palpable.

"No. Of course not. We got together because you're hot. No other reason than that."

"No other reason, hmm?" He cut his eyes at me and moved to the next box. "I almost regret opening that thing now. Didn't think you'd be telling fairytales. I guess I should expect that from a new author." I smiled. The novel I had been working on when we met was in its final editing stages, getting ready for publication soon. It wasn't the life-changing moment I had assumed it would be, but it was still amazing to see my words in print.

"You think your magical journal could tell me when my next gig is coming?" he asked. I sighed. I knew it was a long shot trying to get him to believe what I was saying. I still have trouble believing it myself most days, choosing to leave that part of the story out completely when people want to hear how we met. As far as everyone else knows, there was no journal involved. Even my friends, who had seen the magic in action because of the video I had captured, still had trouble believing it was real.

"Very funny. You don't have to believe me."

"I believe you." He said quickly. I stared at him, narrowing my eyes. "Okay no, I don't."

Last year, when my grandmother gave me this journal, I hadn't been looking for a relationship, let alone looking for anything serious, but clearly, life had something else in mind. All I'd wanted was to work on my novel and make it through the school year with my kids, but I had received so much more. I'd gotten two people to add to my family. The two lights of my life, my love, and my new stepson. These two men had changed so much about how I viewed the world. Now, I moved out of my apartment and into the house with Mekhi and Kellan to complete the family we had started together. For the first time in a long time, I felt like I was truly at home. Mekhi had watched helplessly as I added my touch to everything in the house. Adding even more obnoxious Christmas decorations to the growing collection he had started the year prior.

"Hey El," Kellan had finally managed unglue himself from the PlayStation to get my attention. El was the nickname he had picked when we realized that 'mom' was a little too much too soon. We would get there. Just not yet.

"Yeah?"

"Can we make some of those Christmas cookies again this year? They were so good. Especially the ones you'd made into little Christmas trees."

"Absolutely. I'll run to the store and get the ingredients as soon as I'm done unpacking this box." That was a trick I had learned from many nights of watching Audrey prepare holiday-themed treats for her customers. She had passed on a few tips to me, and I had brought them home, excited to show Kellan and create new traditions for him to look forward to. Even Mekhi had taken part a few times, which had made things even more fun. We all fit so seamlessly into each other's lives.

I walked back over to the journal, feeling nostalgic and wanting to read our story. I had read it so many times over the past year that I had memorized most of the words in it, but that didn't take away from the experience of seeing the words on the page and holding our love story in my hands.

I reached for the book and was surprised to find the page I had just tried to show Mekhi blank. No more swirly script. I flipped to the page before it and the page before that; only to find the entire journal completely empty, as if nothing had been written there at all.

"Mekhi!" I called frantically, flipping through the journal. He came to stand next to me, concern etched in his features.

"What's wrong?" he asked, peering over my shoulder at the

journal.

"It's empty," I said, confused. All the words that had just been written in the journal not even moments ago had vanished, leaving the entire thing full of empty white pages. I stared in disbelief. Mekhi gently took the journal out of my hands and thumbed through the pages himself.

"That's so weird." He mumbled. "Did the pages fall out?"

"No," I replied, checking under and inside the box the journal had been packed in. Our sudden commotion piqued Kellan's interest. He paused the game and turned to us.

"What's wrong?" he asked us, coming closer. "Did you lose something?"

"El's magic journal lost its magic writing," Mekhi absentmindedly flipped through the journal once again.

I glared at him. "I've explained to you what it is and what it does!"

He sighed and then placed the journal on the counter behind me. As soon as his hands touched my sides, I deflated. He pressed his lips to my forehead and wrapped his arms around me when I leaned into his kiss.

"There, there." He said, pretending to be soothing. I could hear the laughter in his voice. "It's just a regular journal." I swatted at him again, but this time, he dodged it. His laughter grew louder and more obnoxious, making me narrow my eyes at him in frustration.

"Stop making fun of me!" I huffed. I regretted trying to explain anything to him. It was enough that my friends would look at me like I'd grown two heads whenever I mentioned the journal. I didn't need my boyfriend looking at me the same way. I was second guessing myself, even though I had seen it happen with my own eyes more than once.

"You're right. I'm sorry, baby." I could tell he still wanted to laugh a little, but he was at least trying not to. Instead of pushing the conversation, I picked up my phone and pulled up the DoorDash app. Instead of trying to convince them, I would just feed them, and we could move on from the conversation. If I hurried, I could add in the ingredients for the cookies and do a double dash. It would save time and allow me to get in the shower before it was time to eat.

"Would Mexican food be okay for dinner? Been craving tacos." I asked, scrolling through the listed restaurants. Mekhi agreed, but Kellan remained silent. I had assumed he had lost interest and gone back to his game, so without looking, I called out to him.

"Kellan, honey. Do you want tacos?" Still no answer. Confused, I looked up from the phone to find him standing in front of the journal, staring down at it in shock. Panic bubbled up in my throat. "Kellan?"

He pointed at the journal. "It's moving!" he whispered.

Mekhi and I both stepped towards him to see what he was talking about. The journal lay on the table untouched, but as we stood there watching it, the pages flipped one by one. Like something seen in a movie, the journal was moving completely on its own. Even having seen it happen before; I was still freaked out to see it happening again.

My grandmother had said that once my story was finished, then it would erase and tell me who to give it to next, but I had been hoping that was just an exaggeration. The three of us stared in shock as it continued to flip, afraid to look away for fear that we would blink and miss whatever was trying to happen. Mekhi reached down and grabbed my hand. I glanced at him quickly and then fixed my eyes back on the impossible phenomenon occurring right in front of us.

The delicate pages of the journal continued to flip, getting faster and faster until it reached the last page. They were moving so quickly that I was worried some pages would rip. Once the pages stopped moving, things were still for a moment and then thick scrawly letters appeared, as if someone was writing them.

"What does it say?" Mekhi asked. His voice was barely above a whisper. I glanced at him, feeling slightly vindicated. Neither of them wanted to get close to it, so I stepped forward until I could see the words clearly on the paper.

This Journal Belongs To: Audrey Bennett.

STAY TUNED FOR BOOK
TWO:

YOU'RE A MEAN ONE, MR. CHEF

About The Author

Lauren Roach is a dog obsessed, true-crime loving, self-proclaimed book nerd that has always dreamed of becoming a published author. While most kids were frolicking in the sun, Lauren chose the path less sweaty and opted for the cool embrace of air conditioning while immersed in a book or busily penning fan fictions about whatever heartthrob boy band was on her radar.

Lauren's literary ambitions took a brief hiatus when she decided to venture into the world of criminal justice, earning both a bachelor's and a master's degree in the field. Even though she has yet to use either one of her degrees for anything career-related, she hopes to maybe use her criminal justice knowledge to one day write a really good mystery plot.

Fast forward to today, Lauren is happily residing in North Carolina with her lovely husband where she starts celebrating Christmas in August and isn't afraid to break out a book in the middle of a social gathering. You can follow her work at

Instagram & Threads: @thebookybabe_
Tik Tok & Bluesky: @thebookybabe
Twitter (X): @LaurenRWrites
Podcast: Lauren's Library Podcast
Website: www.sunflowerrosepublishing.com